"There is nothing cliched about Estleman's use of the English language, which he plays like Isaac Stern would a Stradivarius."

Cincinnati Post

"For readers who can't get enough of Elmore Leonard and Ross Thomas, try Estleman. He's that good."

People

"I think Amos and McGee would understand each other. So Estleman goes on my very short list of the peer group I can read for pleasure."

John D. MacDonald

"The Walker books are among the most enjoyable being written today in the classic private eye field . . . impressively crafted, at once sentimental and cynical."

San Francisco Examiner

THE GLASS HIGHWAY

An Amos Walker Mystery

Loren D. Estleman

FAWCETT CREST · NEW YORK

A Fawcett Crest Book
Published by Ballantine Books
Copyright © 1983 by Loren D. Estleman

Library of Congress Catalog Card Number: 83-8387

ISBN 0-449-21136-3

First published by Houghton Mifflin Company. Reprinted by permission
of Houghton Mifflin Company.

Manufactured in the United States of America

First Ballantine Books Edition: August 1987

To Bob Aeillo:
"He had . . . that look of discipline
you find in the best ones."

1

I SHOWED MY ID TO THE PARKING LOT GUARD, WHO leaned out of his booth for a closer look, then found my name on a list attached to a clipboard and waved me on through. He was wearing a shiny black poncho and a stormtrooper's cap wrapped in clear plastic. The weatherman was predicting rain for Christmas. I drove around a sprawling brick building and parked in the vice president's space on the theory that if he wasn't in by 11:30 A.M. he wasn't coming.

My transportation that year was a three-year-old Oldsmobile Omega, silver-gray, with a speedometer that topped off at eighty, but that was just for traffic checks. The previous owner had used it to run whiskey in Tennessee and wouldn't be needing it for the next ten to fifteen years. My old Cutlass had rolled over and died around 111,000 miles. I was still going last time I checked.

I stepped from a light mist through glass doors into a reception area the size of the maid's bathroom, with orange carpeting and the television station's call letters repeated many times in tasteful gold on brown wallpaper. Holiday music crept in guiltily through a hidden speaker. The guard at the desk, a white-haired marine drill sergeant with glasses and a hearing aid, ran suspicious eyes over me from hat to rubbers and asked for two pieces of identification.

"I'm here to see someone, not cash a check," I said.

He repeated the request deadpan, holding out a leathery palm. I filled it. He read the fine print on the photostat of my investigator's license, then checked the picture on my driver's license against the pores on my face. "You got a credit card?"

I pointed at the first item and said, "You must be kidding."

"Okay." He gave them back. "We got to be careful. Last month some nut strolled in lugging a bomb in his briefcase."

"Was his name Marshall McLuhan?" That bought a blank stare. "Skip it," I said. "You like that music?"

"What music?" He picked up a chocolate telephone, gave my name to someone on the other end, said "Okay" again, and hung up. "Someone'll be out in a minute." He interested himself in a magazine with a girl on the cover in a black leather jacket and nothing else.

It was more like five minutes. I spent them reading the wallpaper. Then a little blonde of about twenty-two, with a boy's haircut and green stuff on her eyelids, appeared through a square arch and said, "Mr. Walker? Follow me, please." She was wearing a yellow pantsuit, which was an improvement over the uniforms I'd been looking at but not much.

We went down a couple of hallways and through a door with an unlit red bulb mounted over it. The room beyond was cavernous, with a gray concrete floor under tangled cable and bright lights glaring down on a man-made oasis against the back wall. There, a blue semi-circular counter stood on a blue dais in front of blue canvas stretched on a frame. A middle-aged man with platinum hair sat shuffling typewritten sheets on an up-holstered cocktail stool behind the counter. His face was broad, tan, and good-looking in the same way that de-partment store dummies are pleasant to look at, and he was wearing a tan suit tailored by a divinity. Next to him, also shuffling papers, sat a woman in her forties got up like a Barbie doll in blond wig and white ruffled blouse.

The set had a cotton-candy look, tethered to reality by a Styrofoam coffee cup at the man's left elbow and a stagehand in baggy gray work clothes leaning on the counter talking to the Barbie doll.

"Mr. Broderick's about to anchor the noon report," whispered my little blonde, and indicated three rows of folding metal chairs set up behind the mammoth caster-mounted cameras. "If you'll sit down he'll be with you in a half hour. Please be quiet while the cameras are rolling."

I took a seat in the back row among a group of college journalism students, which made me feel a little younger than the Fisher Building. So far no one had offered to take my hat and coat.

The floor manager, black-bearded and in sport shirt,

jeans, and headset, asked for silence and started the countdown. Broderick, the platinum-haired newscaster, drained his cup and placed it outside camera range. Someone hit the doomsday music and it was show-time.

Broderick opened with an airline disaster in Seattle, then kicked it over to Barbie, who narrated a film showing the mayor being greeted by the President at the White House before a conference on the plight of the cities, which gave Broderick a chance to report on a clean-up campaign conducted in the Cass Corridor by a group of local Detroit youngsters during the off season in armed robberies. After Barbie did a timely story on Salvation Army Santas—you know the one—Broderick dropped his voice three octaves to describe a little boy's drowning death under the ice in Lake St. Clair. Then he exchanged jokes with the weatherman, who had more rain coming in from Wisconsin and a radar map to prove it in his little blue set across the studio. He called himself a meteorologist.

It was a hell of a show.

When the woman finished putting the Pistons' last basketball game out of its misery, Broderick signed off, waited for the lights to come down, then dumped the papers he'd just reshuffled into a wastebasket behind the counter. Barbie told everyone good-bye and left with the stagehand. She was wearing faded jeans with the frilly blouse. The things you miss when you're planted in front of the TV set.

"Nice work, Sandy," the floor manager told Broderick. "Can you come in an hour early tonight? We got promos to shoot."

4

"You want shirtsleeves or jacket?" Broderick was standing, mopping make-up off his face with a wad of tissue.

"Shirtsleeves, tie loosened. Like you're working on a story or something; you know the routine."

"I never loosen my tie."

"Must look funny in the shower. Oh, and Ray said to tell you not to touch the typewriter while we're shooting. Somebody in the newsroom claimed you broke it last time."

"What do I know from typewriters?" complained the newscaster. "I studied piano."

The little blonde approached Broderick and said something, pointing in my direction. He glanced at me, nodded, and motioned me over. Normally I wouldn't have gone, but I was glad to get off the hard seat.

"Amos Walker?" He clasped my hand firmly. "Sorry I had to call you like a dog, but if those kids thought I was coming over to talk to them I'd never get away."

"Just don't whistle," I said.

"What did you think of the show?"

"The newspapers would have to go some to beat it. For starters they can put the comics on the front page."

The blonde giggled, reminding him she was there. He moved his shoulders uneasily. "We'll talk in my office. They gave me one, Lord knows why."

"Something tells me you don't write your own copy." We were walking now, leaving the girl behind. I was watching my feet to avoid tripping over cables.

He shook his head. "I hear some TV newsmen do,

but I've never met one. God doesn't give out good looks, a deep voice, *and* brains that often. If you tell anyone I said that I'll deny it.''

"They won't hear it from me."

His office had a spacious airiness that was completely spoiled when we walked in. Although it was large enough to contain much more, it had a desk, a sofa, and a steel bookcase stuffed with review copies of hardcover books. The station didn't do book reviews. A window looked out on the low buildings and latticework overpasses of suburban Detroit, giving my host as true a picture of the city as Hitler's bunker offered of World War II. I shucked the outerwear and we took up the classic positions, he on his side of the desk, I on mine. The desk was chromium and pressed sawdust under a plastic woodgrain veneer, without drawers or front or side panels. It had legs.

Sandy Broderick looked older and slimmer when he wasn't under studio lights. His cheeks were hollow and scored. The tan was real, not just make-up, but it was the kind you get in those tanning places that charge by the hour for something you can get from the sun all day for free if you're willing to wait for summer. He had a country club build under the jacket. At two and a half yards a day plus expenses, I seemed well within his budget.

"I lunch with Barry Stackpole from the *News*," he told me. "Barry says you can be counted on to work twenty-five hours for twenty-four hours' pay and not tell anyone about it who shouldn't be told."

"Barry's a bright guy," I said.

"He also says you can sometimes be counted on to

talk yourself into more trouble than you can climb out of without artillery support.''

''What's he know?''

''I'm not concerned with what he said. What does concern me is how much trouble you have to be in before you use me to bail you out.''

I set fire to a Winston and dropped the match, still burning, into a copper ashtray on the desk. ''Why don't you tell me what the job is, and then I'll tell you how likely I am to get into a hole over it and how deep.''

He gave his head another shake. His hair was sprayed hard as a carp and didn't move. I wondered if the color was real. ''If I tell you, it'd be the same as hiring you. What about references?''

''Don't have any.''

He arched his eyebrows the way he had when the weatherman told him it was as miserable out as Scrooge's disposition. I said, ''Not the kind you can use, judges and cops and like that. I run a one-man agency as yet innocent of an urgent call from the bench, and cops and P.I.'s are natural enemies. They'd give me a good recommendation like I'd wrestle a skunk. There's a lieutenant in Homicide who might be called a friend if you stretch the term till it creaks, but we generally try to stay out of each other's back pockets. I'll stand on what Barry says, the first part anyway.''

I waited, smoking and flicking ash into the tray. Traffic hummed past on the Lodge. It was still misting out, and gray as old underwear. At length Broderick stirred and placed his forearms on the desk's glossy top.

His eyes searched mine—pale, colorless eyes that looked blue on camera.

"It's my son, Walker," he said. "I want you to find Bud for me while he's still alive."

I snatched one last drag, ditched the butt, and excavated my little notepad. My memory for details had deteriorated since my thirty-third birthday.

2

"BUD'S TWENTY," HE BEGAN. "MY WIFE GOT CUS-tody when we divorced six years ago, then she remarried and moved here with him and her new husband. I haven't seen him since. He's one reason I took this job; the money's not that much better here and the climate stinks." He inclined his head toward the waterworks outside.

"California, right?" I prompted.

"Sacramento. Does it show?"

"Like a pink flamingo in a parking lot."

"I'll adapt. Anyway, when I got out here and dropped in on my ex-wife—"

"I wish I had that reunion on film."

He looked at me with new interest. "You too?"

"Yeah."

"Bitch, isn't it?"

I agreed that it was a bitch. That made us war buddies. He relaxed a notch.

"Her name's Sharon. When I visited her in Grosse Pointe, she said she was just considering calling me in

California. She hadn't seen or heard from our son in almost a month. He took an apartment in Rawsonville last year when he landed a job at the Ford plant there. He came home to visit every couple of weeks or so and sometimes stayed over on weekends. When he failed to show up or call two weekends in a row, Sharon tried to call him. She got a recording saying his phone had been disconnected. She drove out there and spoke to his landlord. He told her Bud had moved out about ten days before, just after he got laid off from the plant. She hadn't even known he'd been laid off. I dropped in while she was vacillating between notifying the police and calling me. That was yesterday. I called you as soon as I got your name from Barry.''

"Did you check with Unemployment?''

"They haven't heard from him either.''

"The cops are good at this sort of thing,'' I said. "They have the manpower and the facilities. When you hire me, me is all you get.''

"Barry says that's plenty.'' He rubbed a nicely manicured thumb over what might have been an irregularity in the desk's plastic surface if it had had irregularities. "There's something else.''

"There usually is.''

"The man Sharon married is named Esterhazy, Charles Esterhazy. He has a grown daughter, Fern, who lives with them. She's been married and divorced twice. She's what we used to call fast before the sexual revolution rescued us from Victorian bondage.'' He made one of those faces newscasters call wry. "She introduced Bud into her circle of acquaintances, specifically a girl named Paula Royce, who is four years older than

Bud. They were seeing quite a bit of each other before he disappeared, Sharon says."

I wrote down the name. If I had a nickel for every young man who vanished that year without some girl being tied up in it somewhere I'd have a nickel. "Let me guess. The girl's disappeared too."

Someone tapped lightly on the door. Broderick said something pithy under his breath, then raised his voice. "Come in."

The short-haired blonde in yellow entered carrying a manila envelope and tipped its contents out under his nose. They were six eight-by-ten photographs of Broderick interviewing someone on the steps of the City-County Building. They looked stagey as hell. "Ray wants your okay on these before we send them out," she said apologetically.

"Tell him they're fine." He returned them to the envelope without a glance and gave it back.

She hesitated with her hands on the item. "Are you coming by tonight?"

"I'm busy, Marlene."

She flushed slightly and left.

"The girl's the dead end," he told me, when the door was closed. "No one knows where she lives, not even Fern. They only saw each other at parties, she says. Sharon didn't approve. She met her once at Bud's apartment. She thinks the girl's on drugs."

"What kind?" I asked. "Coke? Heroin? Pills?"

"She doesn't even know for sure it's dope. It's just the way the girl acted, like she was a quarter-beat behind. And Fern isn't talking, at least not to her stepmother. They get along great, those two. Like bitch dogs.''

"You think Paula Royce may acquaint your son with the wonderful world of oblivion?''

"The possibility exists,'' he said. "My ex-wife has never suffered from what you would call an overdeveloped sense of responsibility. She has little enough of her own to have passed any on to Bud, and if Fern is any example I think the same can be said of Sharon's current husband.''

I frowned at my notes. "You're afraid if you tell the cops and they find your son they'll bust him for possession, is that it?''

The newscaster shifted his position twice, ending up where he had started. Then he drew a folded sheet from an inside breast pocket and handed it to me. "There's a copy of that on every editor's desk in southeastern Michigan.''

I unfolded the sheet. It was a news release typed under the station's letterhead, announcing that Sandy Broderick, the dean of Detroit newsmen, would present a weekly segment on narcotics abuse on the 6:00 and 11:00 P.M. news reports beginning next Monday.

"There's a chance of syndication and maybe even a network spot if it clicks,'' he explained. "Police officers love to hear themselves talk. If it gets out my own son is humping a junkie—if that's what she is—and possibly dropping the stuff himself, they'll hear the laughter back in Sacramento. If he ODs and pops up at the morgue I'll be lucky to land a spot on an afternoon bowling show.''

"Ungrateful little bastard.''

His fingers hesitated in the midst of refolding the release, then resumed. He put it away. "My son was fourteen last time I saw him. He was into bugs and baseball. I have no idea what sort of man he's become. Naturally I'm concerned about him"—his voice dropped three octaves—"but you can't expect that concern to be as great as if I had raised him all these years. Instead, I've been building a career. I won't let Sharon take that away from me like she did Bud."

"Is Bud his real first name?"

He nodded. "And he hung on to Broderick, in spite of Esterhazy's attempts to adopt him. He's named after my late father."

"That explains why he named you Sandy." I tapped my pencil on my knee. "If I find him, what do you want me to do? He's an adult. If I bring him to you kicking I'm a kidnaper, and to be square there's a substantial list of things I'd rather do than try wrestling a healthy twenty-year-old back to Daddy. That job's for the fellows in uniform and they have nothing to fear from me."

"I'm not asking for that. I don't want that. I wouldn't know what to do with him if you did. I just want to know where he is so I can get in touch with him." He uncapped a fat green fountain pen, scribbled a telephone number on the top sheet of a pad on the desk, tore it off, and gave it to me. "That's my home number. It's unlisted. When you find him, call. Maybe his father can talk some sense into him. It's clear his mother can't."

"It's your money," I said, tucking the scrap inside my pad. "Speaking of which."

He produced a flat wallet and counted out ten hundreds. "Is a thousand dollars an adequate retainer?"

I allowed as it was and scooped the crisp new bills into my own tired wallet like a shoplifter cleaning out a jewelry display. "I need more on Bud. Skills, hobbies, personality, friends. And a recent picture if you've got one."

"You'll have to get all that from Sharon. He's a stranger to me, as I said." He gave me her telephone number and address in Grosse Pointe. I took it down. He rose. "Report when you have something. Not here, if you can avoid it. I wouldn't have met you here if this weren't urgent and I could have been home last night. The studio brass threw a party to welcome me to the station."

"I thought your eyes looked bloodshot." I stood and grasped his proffered hand.

He smiled for the first time since I met him. "As the Indian said to the cowboy, 'You should see them from this side.' Bring me good news."

Blonde Marlene was brushing correction fluid onto a sheet in her IBM machine when I hit the reception room outside. I got out a cigarette and tapped it against the back of my hand. "He's all yours."

"Not yet, but he will be," she said, and flashed white teeth between glossed lips. We wished each other merry Christmas. She had a nice smile. It was a shame about the haircut and the gunk on her eyelids.

IN THE PARKING LOT THE RAIN HAD TURNED TO SLEET. Tiny icicles shattered against my face and crackled like frying bacon when they struck asphalt. A fat bald guy in a trenchcoat with vice president stamped all over his rosy features was giving my car the evil eye in the space with someone's name on it. He had the lot guard with him. I walked past them trailing smoke and unlocked the door on the driver's side. Fatso waddled forward.

"I just wanted to meet the reason I had to park half a mile down the pike." His voice squeaked when he raised it. "I was about to have you towed away. Can't you read? This is my space."

"Not anymore it isn't," I said, starting the motor. "Watch those long lunches next job."

His face looked a little gray in the rearview mirror as I was leaving. Not the guard's, though. I hadn't seen a grin that broad since the last time I paid my bar tab.

I ORDERED A HAM AND CHEESE SANDWICH AND A GLASS of water in a diner on Evergreen and had them half consumed before I remembered that I could afford better. So I gave the guy behind the counter a five-spot and told him to keep the change. He made me stay while he counted the whiskers in Lincoln's beard. When he was finished I asked for change and decided not to eat there again soon.

Sleet rattled against the diner's front window like skeletal fingers. I dropped two dimes into a pay telephone near the door and pecked out Sharon Esterhazy's number. She answered after one ring. Her speech had a thin, wound-up quality, like an excited Chihuahua or a Ronstadt album played at 75 RPM. At first she thought I was Bud calling to tell her where he was. I disappointed her as gently as possible and arranged a 3:00 P.M. meeting at her house. When I asked if her stepdaughter would be there too, she said, "Who knows?" laughed a little too gaily, and clicked off.

Pronging the receiver, I had a flash of that black feeling you get when you've just started reading a book and you realize you're going to hate it. But the feeling passed quickly and I blamed it on the rotten weather. Premonitions are like horoscopes. If you take them too seriously you wind up doing nothing. I headed for my bank.

3

THE HOUSE WAS A BRICK COLONIAL AROUND THE COR-
ner from Grosse Pointe's brisk downtown section, two
stories high with white-shuttered windows, scrolls on
the columns, and a widow's walk from where you might
see water if you stood on tiptoe and used your imagi-
nation. The lawn was big enough for softball, but right
now there was a puddle in the middle wide enough to
turn a cabin cruiser around in, proving that even the rich
suffer during the winter; it was just a question of degrees. I parked in front of a garage that had been a
carriage house in gentler times, checked my rubbers for
cow flop, and went up and rang the doorbell. It made a
noise like coins spilling. It would.

"Something I can do for you, brown eyes?"

If she was less than six feet tall, I had shrunk. Our
eyes were almost level—hers were gray, like raw silver—and when I managed to glance down I saw that she
was wearing loafers, not high heels. She was also wearing slacks and a matching top of some clinging, glittery
green material that the tailor had run out of at mid-calf

and -forearm. They call them lounging pajamas. I call them trouble, especially with her inside of them at this time of day. Her hair was full, waist-length, and very red. It looked natural, but I'm no Sassoon. Her lips were painted crimson to match the long nails she had curled around the edge of the door. She had pale skin. She wouldn't see much sun dressed like that. She was half-way through her twenties.

"Christmas shopping?" Her tone knew me.

"Why did I know you'd say that?" I asked. "You'd be Fern. You look like an exotic plant."

"We both feed on decay. You're the sleuth who called Sharon about Bud."

I grinned. "It's the gum soles, right?"

"It's the gum soles, wrong. I've hired enough P.I.'s to be able to identify the animal. You don't enter a room till you've appraised all the furniture and found the laundry mark on the drapes. Sharon's busy making herself presentable. You may as well come in; you're in for a long wait."

"Meow."

We went into a living room with beige silk on the walls, some chairs and a sofa upholstered in brown leather, and a baby grand piano that was there just to hold up an African violet in a steel pot. Other potted plants stood along the base of the rear wall, which was all window looking out on a young maple with a wire fence around it, and beyond it the other houses in the neighborhood. The furniture was good for ten grand, by the way, and the drapes were cleaned at a place called Frawley's on Kercheval.

"You'd get catty too, after you lived with the queen

as long as I have,'' said Fern, hanging my coat and hat in a closet the size of my kitchen.

I left my rubbers in a puddle on the hall floor. ''Why not move out?''

''What'll I pay the rent with, my good looks?''

''It's been done. I was thinking more along the lines of a job. You look healthy.''

''And blow my amateur standing? No thanks. I'll take my chances with Nefertiti, there, at least until I find my next husband. Are you interested?''

''What's in it for me?'' I sank into one of the leather armchairs.

She looked at me, sizing up the goods, then folded herself across one padded arm and planted a lingering one on my mouth. She smelled of the usual cosmetics and that scent the female of the species exudes when she's in season. When it was over she straightened, hoisted a bucketful of hair back over one shoulder, and waited.

''Yeah,'' I said. ''But I bet you can't bake.''

She made a hoarse noise that might have been laughter and offered me a cigarette from a carved box on the glass-topped coffee table. I held up one of my own. She selected one for herself, removed an Aqua-filter from a package on the table, and coupled them. Everybody's trying to quit but me. She used a silver table lighter to start both of ours and went over and sat down on the sofa. She moved her legs around a good deal getting comfortable. They gleamed like stretched satin below the pajama cuffs.

''There's no profit in hooking a private eye.'' Smoke trailed out her nostrils. ''The honest ones boil their shoes for lunch and the crooked ones are all greasy to the touch. When I marry again it's going to be to someone with his name in the Social Register and one foot in the intensive care ward at Detroit Receiving.''

"For shame," I chided. "ERA and all."

"I never asked to be liberated. Besides, any constitutional amendment that can't pass without bribery and coercion—or with it, for that matter—can't be that good."

"Now that we're such good friends, what can you tell me about Paula Royce?"

Her eyes glittered. "I must be losing it. There was a time when I could make a man forget what business he was in for hours at a stretch."

"I bet you still could—if you tried. What about Paula Royce?"

"I put on the PJ's and everything. When Sharon told me a pair of pants was on its way—"

"You're not half the slut you like to think you are. There's a time and place for the sex stuff, and these ain't them. Paula Royce."

"You're an icy son of a bitch," she said. "I bet if I cut you you'd bleed Freon gas. I'd like to try and thaw you out one of these nights." Her eyes smoked over.

"Paula—" I started to say. She held up a hand.

"Okay, okay. You don't have to smack me in the kisser with a salami. I can tell you all I know about Paula while waiting for a traffic light to change. We only knew each other to say hello at parties. A sweet-tempered girl, I think. Quiet. Petite, if you like those cute French words. A brunette. All things I'm not."

"Where'd you meet her?"

"At a party, where else? Don't ask me whose. One's pretty much like another. I guess it was about a year ago."

"Who brought her?"

"I think she brought herself. I never saw her come in with anyone, there or the other places. If she ever left with someone I didn't see that either, probably because I'd left by that time with someone myself."

"Was Bud there?"

"Mnm-mm." She was sucking on the filter. "They didn't get together until three or four months ago. It was a do at Rhett Grissom's. My date couldn't make it at the last minute, so Bud offered to take me. He knew I try never to miss one of Rhett's parties. The poor dear was so gallant."

"How long have you been talking about your step-brother in the past tense?"

She raised a pair of rather thick eyebrows. "Did I do that? Maybe it's because he was so easy to forget. Damn it, there I go again. It's hard to imagine him existing at all when you're not in the room with him. Maybe that's what attracted Paula. She was the same way."

"I hear your stepmother thinks she's a doper."

"She should talk." It came out in a bitter rush of smoke.

I imitated her raised-eyebrow expression.

She said, "Sharon pops so many pills it's a wonder she has a chance to eat. Pills to wake up, pills to fall asleep, pills to lose weight, pills to gain it back. When she farts the room smells like a hospital ward. Paula's nowhere near the doper she is. Probably not as much."

"You're saying Paula does pills."

"Who doesn't these days, outside Christian Science?" She stabbed out her butt in an onyx ashtray on the coffee table. The butt wasn't half smoked. "Sharon thinks because she gets hers on a prescription and we get ours from a bowl at a party she's holy and we're bound for hell. Her doctor's just a high-priced pusher with a diploma."

"Were there pills at Rhett Grissom's party?"

She started to answer. Then she smiled and placed the tip of a crimson-nailed forefinger against her upper lip. "For a minute there I forgot you're a detective," she said. "It's the brown eyes. You ought to have them registered."

I dredged up my pad and pencil. "That's Rhett as in Butler, G-R-I-S-S-O-M?"

"Self-incrimination, darling." She patted my knee and stood. "I have a date coming by at four. Excuse me while I slip into something a little less comfortable."

"Who for, you or your date?"

She smiled again with her red-red lips and brushed her fingers along my jawline as she sashayed past. I twisted around in my chair to watch her leave. She passed another woman coming through the doorway from another room. They said nothing to each other.

"Mr. Walker? I'm Sharon Esterhazy."

I got up and shook hands with a woman six inches shorter than her stepdaughter. She wore a cream-colored blouse with puffed sleeves, tucked into a brown flaring skirt cut to mask a slight middle-age weight shift, and her hair, arranged in a kind of pageboy, was that shade of blond that dark-haired women adopt to hide the gray as they grow older. She had on too much eye make-up, and from her nose to her mouth there were deep lines that powder couldn't conceal. Her smile was as tight as a fist. Her hand felt cold.

I moved my inner dial to Tranquil Charm and said, "Thanks for agreeing to see me, Mrs. Esterhazy. I didn't give you much notice."

"Nonsense. Do I look like a busy woman? I'm just another one of those useless society butterflies you read about."

She made me a drink offer, which I declined, then waved me back into my seat and perched on the edge of the sofa with her rather thick ankles crossed and her hands folded in her lap, consciously avoiding the still-warm spot where Fern had been sitting. She looked about as much like a society butterfly as I look like Boris Karloff. I kept hearing nervous Chihuahuas in her speech.

"I'll be honest with you, Mr. Walker," she said. "I wasn't in favor of hiring you. It was Sandy's idea. I think it's a police matter and I may still call them. My husband pays taxes for just that privilege."

I put out my cigarette next to Fern's. "How does Mr. Esterhazy feel about that?"

"He's left the decision to Sandy and me. He says that Bud's our son and that he shouldn't interfere."

"What does your husband do for a living?"

"He's an investment counselor. He built his own firm from the ground up, and now he employs twenty-three people. He's a self-made man, unlike most of our neighbors."

Her tone was defensive. When a wife talks that way

about her husband you get to wondering how many squashed toes he's left behind. "Did he and Bud get along?"

"Why do you ask?" The little dogs were yapping now. Her back was as straight as a pistol shot.

"I'm just establishing a background," I explained. "Bud was over fourteen when you remarried, old enough to have a sense of father that wouldn't transfer easily to a relative stranger. I understand he wouldn't let Mr. Esterhazy adopt him. Whenever a young person drops out of sight I have to wonder if family friction was a contributing factor."

"Well, you can stop wondering. As you say, Bud was too old to accept Charles as his father, but they got along very well. Bud called him by his first name."

And Fern called her stepmother by hers. But I took a passed ball. "It was just a test shot. Bud wasn't living at home when he disappeared, so it seemed unlikely. But the police would have asked the same question. What sort of man is your son? Your stepdaughter says he's quiet."

"A mortar burst would be quiet compared to her," she said dryly. "Bud's a normal twenty-year-old boy. He was on his high school debating team, played baseball, and dated, not always girls I approved of. I don't imagine that's unusual. He has good manners, which I suppose Fern might mistake for shyness, never having had any of her own. I wanted him to attend college, but he wanted to take some time out to think about it. He lived here for a year while he went to job interviews and filled out applications. Then he was hired for the line at the Ford Rawsonville plant. As soon as he had some money in the bank, he moved out to be near his work. I didn't want him to. What mother would? I was hoping he'd save the money for tuition. He's got too much upstairs to spend the rest of his life tightening nuts."

"What about his interests outside of his job? Does he have hobbies?"

"Sports and reading. He belonged to a local softball club, but he gave that up when he went to work. I think he liked books better anyway. Action stories, mostly. Spy fiction. I tried to get him interested in Hemingway and Fitzgerald, but he always came back to that Ludlum person."

I pretended to make a note of that. "Paula Royce."

Her jaw clenched. "If anything's happened to Bud and she's responsible I'll kill her."

The air in the room had changed. I moved my shoulders around under my jacket. Now I knew where Sandy Broderick had picked up the mannerism. "Tell me about the time you saw her at your son's apartment."

"She wasn't living there. Understand that." Her hands twisted in her lap. "The day he makes that kind of arrangement, if he ever does, it won't be with someone like her. I had nothing to do and it was a nice day to get out—it was October, the color was peaking—so I drove over there for a visit. They were having an early dinner, something Bud had cooked. That surprised me, because he'd never cooked anything before, not while he was living here, in any case. She was very rude. She said I should have called first. Maybe that's true, but it seems to me that was for Bud to say. And I'm sure she was on drugs. Her speech was slurred, kind of drunken, except she wasn't drunk. I could tell the difference."

"What did you do?"

"What could I do? I left. Bud was polite, but I could see that the situation was making him nervous. I expected him to call later and explain, or apologize the next time we saw each other. But he never mentioned it. A month later he stopped coming to visit. I suppose Sandy's told you the rest."

I leaned on routine. Did Bud behave oddly during his last couple of visits? He seemed preoccupied, but not upset. A mother notices such things. Had she talked with her son's friends? None or them had seen him since he took up with the Royce girl; can't imagine why they'd lie. I asked for some names and wrote them down. I mentioned a picture. She went into another room for a minute and returned with a five-by-seven black-and-white portrait in a silver frame of a hefty youth with hair like wet sand smiling frozenly at the camera. Sandy Broderick's eyes looked out at me from Sharon Esterhazy's face.

"He had it taken last summer," she explained. "I'd told him I hadn't had a picture of him since his high school graduation."

I took it apart and gave her back the frame. Then I played my wild card.

"Do you know a Rhett Grissom?"

Her brow creased. "The boy who gave the party where Bud met the girl? He lives here in Grosse Pointe with his parents, though I think they're in Hawaii. He didn't go with them. But he's not a friend of Bud's. Do you think he knows where Bud is?"

"He might know someone who does. What's his address?"

She gave it to me. While I was writing, an automobile horn blasted in the street out front. It sounded like money.

"That's Fern's date. When I was her age, young men rang the bell." She got up, smoothing her skirt.

I did the same, minus the skirt part. "Maybe this one knows Fern will come running no matter how she's called."

"She'll be glad to hear you said that. She's been playing the part of the scarlet woman so long she's beginning to believe it herself."

At the front door, Sharon Esterhazy got my hat and coat out of the closet and I climbed into them. I put on the rubbers. "Thanks for your help. I'll call if anything else occurs to me."

Her face looked pinched and old in the gray light sifting in through the transom. "May I ask what my ex-husband is paying you to look for our son?"

"A thousand dollars. That's a four-day retainer." I opened the door. Someone sitting behind the wheel of a black Corvette parked across the end of the driveway perked up, then saw me, and settled back into his slump.

"I might have guessed," she said. "If Sandy were trapped in an alley and a truck were bearing down on him, he'd throw money at it."

I got out of there.

4

THE PARTY IN THE 'VETTE OBSERVED MY APPROACH
down the walk through a pair of pink-tinted sunglasses.
No one in those parts had seen the sun since November.
His face was suety and he was wearing a toupee that
had cost him some change ten years ago, but it hadn't
gone gray like his sideburns. It looked like an angry
black cat crouching on his head. He had on a blue lei-
sure suit over a white turtleneck, young man's clothes.
He was upwards of forty.

I didn't realize the engine was running until I was
standing next to it. He could have heard the dashboard
clock humming if he had one that worked, and I bet he
had. "Here for Fern?" I fed my face a butt.

He had slid over as far as the console allowed and
rolled down the passenger's window to catch my philosophy. He looked at the question from both sides, then
said, "Yeah," cautiously.

"Hope you brought training wheels."

He was still turning that one over when the lady came
out of the house. Purple dress showed under the hem of

a long gray coat with a high waist, and under that black leather boots with needle heels. She was still too short for professional basketball. "I see you two have met."

"We had word," I said.

She didn't let it puzzle her long. "Ernie's taking me to a party."

"Where at, the intensive care ward?"

"Who is this guy?" demanded Ernie. He hadn't budged except to flip up the lock button on the passenger's side. Galahads like him are as rare as zippers these days.

"His name's Walker." She was looking at me with that canary-feather smile. "He says he's a detective."

"Oh, yeah? Well, no money changed hands." Ernie was a card.

"What would someone like you be doing when he's not sleuthing?" she asked.

"I collect bruises."

"Hey, you hitting on this guy on my time?"

She ignored him. "I guess your number's in the book. I may use it some time."

"I may answer." I opened the door for her.

She got in and looked up at me. "I'm serious. Maybe we can have a drink. Or something."

"Give my neck a break and leave the heels at home."

Her smile got too heavy for her. She let go of it and swung the door shut. I barely got my fingers out of the way. Ernie tried to splash me with mud from his rear wheel, but I stepped back and saved everything above the knees. I stood on the frozen wet grass, watching them roar away and getting rained on and smoking and sounding the depths of my ability to say the wrong thing.

WINDSOR'S SULLEN SKYLINE GLOWERED ACROSS A GUN-metal-colored Lake St. Clair, its surface sliced by wind and sleet into timid breakers that touched the Grissoms' backyard and withdrew to tell the others. The house, a Victorian jumble of gables, turrets, and rusty pikes meant to discourage seagulls from roosting on the roof, overlooked a private wharf at the end of a paved cul-de-sac off East Jefferson. Outbuildings included a garage, boat house, and a little hut where the guests could change out of their wet swimsuits into dry martinis. The place didn't even have a heliport.

The guy tinkering in front of the garage didn't hear me pull up and get out. He wouldn't have heard a Soviet first strike on the garage. He had the hood up on a bright red snowmobile and was listening to the chainsaw motor whine.

"Expecting snow?" I shouted at his bent back.

He snapped up like a Vietcong snare and whirled to face me. You'd go some miles before you found some-one who looked less like Clark Gable. Long, dirty-blond hair thinning at the crown and hanging limply behind his ears, long acne-scarred face and drooping mous-tache, long body and legs in fleece-lined denim jacket and dirty jeans, brown cowboy boots scuffed at the toes and splitting at the soles. Sharp eyes under heavy lids. About thirty. He saw me standing with my coat hanging open and my hands in my pants pockets, and he relaxed. He had a heavy wrench in one hand.

"It's got to come sometime," he said. "When it does I'll be ready. Is it me you want?"

"It is if you're Rhett Grissom."

"That depends on whether you're a cop or not."

"Do I look like one?"

"You don't look like someone who isn't one. You got ID?"

"If I showed it to you it wouldn't mean anything. I'm private. You've heard Bud Broderick is missing."

"I didn't even know he was here to begin with." He picked up a white cotton rag and wiped his hands. His hands were clean.

"He was, as a matter of fact. Right here. He came to one of your famous parties with his stepsister a few months back. Fern Esterhazy. She introduced him to another guest, Paula Royce. They hit it off."

"Man, I don't even remember who came to my party last Saturday night."

"It's the pills. You should lay off them awhile."

His lids flickered. "What pills?"

Somehow I had known those would be the next words out of his mouth.

"The Royce girl was a regular at your bashes," I said. "We both know she didn't come for the good food and stimulating conversation. I won't send you over. The cops don't listen to me anyway. What I want to know is if you were supplying her the rest of the time, and if you weren't, who was." I stopped to swallow. "Cut the motor, will you? I'm starting to feel my tonsils."

He mouthed two words that were drowned out by the racket and bent over the motor, gripping his wrench. I reached past his shoulder and gave the throttle on the handlebar a flirt. The machine squirted forward. Grissom lost his balance and pitched face first onto the wet asphalt driveway, but not before the vehicle tried to climb the closed garage door, stalled, and fell over. They heard the noise in Lansing.

"Son of a bitch!" howled Grissom, swiping the wrench at my shin. I hopped over it, kicked his supporting arm out from under him, and planted a foot on his wrist. I found a place for the other foot on the back of his head. Teeth ground on asphalt.

"Paula Royce," I said. "Were you supplying her?"

He braced his free hand on the driveway again and tried to throw me off. I kicked it again with the foot I had on his head and took up the earlier position as his chest struck ground, emptying his lungs with an animal grunt.

"Her supplier." I leaned on his head.

He made an unintelligible sound of acquiescence. When it soared to a pleading whine, I got off and pulled him up by his collar. When he was on his knees he swung at me with the wrench. I caught his arm and twisted it behind his back as I lifted him to his feet. The tool tinkled to earth.

I said, "Let's go inside."

He steered quite easily when I heaved up on the arm and pushed. At the back door of the house I asked, "You want to open it, or should I do it with your head?"

He wanted to open it. I let go and we stepped into a large kitchen furnished with an antique table and chairs, wood-burning stove, maple chopping block not much bigger than the GM Building, and crowing roosters on the curtains. A modern refrigerator and a microwave oven looked like things that had dropped through a time warp. The stove was working; the temperature inside was thirty degrees warmer and the smell of burning wood made me nostalgic for a childhood I had never had. I deposited him in one of the chairs at the table, checked out the pantry, and poked my head into the next room, a big dining room with a chandelier and one of those long tables you see in Bugs Bunny cartoons. They were deserted.

"Where's the butler, out walking the parakeet?"

"We haven't had a butler since I was six." He spat out grit and blood from his chewed lip. "The maid's gone shopping or something."

I twirled a chair and mounted it like Randolph Scott, folding my arms across the back. "Well?"

He worked his sore arm and grimaced. "I wasn't supplying her. I don't know who was. Or is. I haven't seen her in weeks. She didn't show up Saturday night. If this Bud guy did I don't know it."

I showed him the picture. He glanced at it and shook his head. I put it away. "Where'd you know the Royce girl from?"

"Nowhere. She just started showing up at parties. Not just mine. Wherever there were pills, come to think of it. Just another crasher. Man, you almost broke my fucking arm, you know that?"

"If I wanted to I would've. Who supplies you?"

He looked at me, and he didn't have heavy lids anymore. He didn't have any kind of lids at all. "Forget it. Break an arm if you want. Break both of them. I got lockjaw."

"Stop being dramatic. They won't kill you, not for dropping a name to a peeper. Ever been busted?"

"What for? You're the one broke my snow toy. You going to pay for that, by the way?"

"Ask Mommy and Daddy to buy you a new one. I'm talking about pushing prescription drugs."

"Once. My freshman year at college. Hell, that's twelve years ago. Passed water."

"It'll float you straight into Jackson if you fall again."

He showed me his teeth. He had gravel in his moustache. "My father eats lunch with the commissioner."

"It's an election year," I reminded him. "You can't spend lunch at the polls. If the cops in Grosse Pointe are like the cops in Detroit—and they all drink the same brand of beer and root for the same football teams—they're watching you now. Your folks are in Hawaii. You've probably already started stocking up for this Saturday night. Suppose some solid citizen drops a word in some officer's ear that a search of the Grissom place just might make his whole week. Today's Wednesday. They're serving turkey roll down at the Wayne County Jail. You'll like it. I don't think."

He showed me more teeth. He slid into a slouch and crossed his long legs, bouncing the one on top. He rat-a-tat-tatted long slender fingers with ragged nails on the table. He whistled "Judy in Disguise" through his teeth. Then he uncrossed his legs and sat up and stared at the bridge of my nose. He said: "Moses True."

"Try again. True's strictly Twelfth Street. They wouldn't let him walk his dogs here."

"Come on, man. How'd I know his name otherwise?"

I beat a tattoo of my own on the tabletop. "He was

still working downtown last Christmas. Who'd he replace?''

"That name you don't have to pry out of me. Johnny Ralph Dorchet.''

Some names trigger instant responses. That one put me in front of my television set around New Year's Day, watching news footage of three bagged corpses being wheeled into a county fast-wagon from an apartment on Erskine. One of the corpses had belonged to Johnny Ralph Dorchet. The world was suddenly more interesting. I swung off the chair and leaned my face down close to Grissom's.

"True still on Twelfth?''

"How the hell should I know? He doesn't deal at his place. He calls me and we meet different places.'' He pulled in his chin to avoid collision. I pushed in closer. Some things you never forget from basic training.

"If he's expecting me I'll come back and watch you eat your telephone circuit by circuit.''

"You won't tell him where you got the name, will you? You say he won't kill me, but that leaves a lot of room for what he will do.''

"Frankly, Rhett, I don't give a damn.''

He wrinkled his nose. "Oh, funny. I heard that one before.''

I went out to my bucket. The snowmobile was lying on its side, its headlight smashed and one ski broken. The garage door might have been scuffed.

Dusk was gathering in corners. Beyond Lake St. Clair, which was as black as a new galosh, early lights spangled the Canadian side. The orange running lights of a squat ore carrier crawled south toward River Rouge and the iron foundry at the Ford plant. Nocturnal things like Moses True would be getting up about now, staring into the closet and wondering whether to put on the coat with the ermine trim or the purple vest. I decided to postpone going to see him until morning. You don't hunt vampires at night.

5

HOME IS A THREE-ROOM ORANGE CRATE ON HAM-
tramck's west side, not far from where the iron ball
was making sawdust out of the historic homes, shops,
and church of Poletown in the name of General Mo-
tors and the city administration's mantra, Total Employment. First, GM had dangled the carrot of a new
Cadillac plant under the mayor's nose, then the black
knight of Eminent Domain had charged in with token
payments for the dreams of lifetimes, and finally those
stubborn residents who had refused to leave were
burned and trashed out by vandals, none of whom the
city police seemed able to apprehend. The case against
Eminent Domain had gone to court twice and lost.
Both courts were located in Detroit. So the wreckers
came and the mayor was re-elected by his customary
landslide and everyone was waiting for GM's next
move. And waiting.

I broiled a steak for supper and ate it off a tray in
front of the television set watching Sandy Broderick and
the Six O'Clock News. He and the Barbie doll and a

pansy in a blazer doing a live minicam report from Joe Louis Arena were kicking around preparations for a rock concert, scheduled for January in the crumbling white elephant taxpayers hadn't finished paying for. All the newscasters agreed that the event would be good for Detroit. The Chamber of Commerce spent a lot of advertising dollars on local TV.

When the news ended I had a choice of three animated Christmas specials and a Pistons' basketball game. I turned off the set and put a record on my economy stereo—just two speakers, no tape deck or filters or laser can openers—bought myself a double Scotch from the bottle I reserved for guests and sat down and listened to Lee Wiley singing about the street of dreams. The Scotch tasted like more. When the glass was full a second time I held it up, admiring the pure copper color of the liquid. It looked smug. It didn't know about pills and people like Rhett Grissom and Moses True and that it was obsolete. I drank it and turned in when the record was through.

The weather wasn't doing anything at all when I got up next morning. The temperature had risen enough during the night to thaw the street in front of my house, but the wind had come up and swept away the puddles, giving everything outside the window a scoured, uninhabited drabness like a faded black-and-white photograph of an evacuated city. It matched my mood.

I had orange juice and coffee for breakfast. Chewing hurts my head after a quadruple-Scotch night. It didn't used to, but then neither did a lot of things. I exercised some of the stiffness out of my joints, showered, and left the house at seven wearing my dancing pumps. At half-past I was where I wanted to be on Twelfth Street.

The signs said Rosa Parks Boulevard now, after the black woman who had started it all by refusing to sit in the back of the bus, but aside from that it hadn't changed since that sweaty Sunday morning in July 1967 when a bottle shattered the rear window of a police car parked in front of the Economy Printing Company and triggered the week-long rioting that had killed forty-three people and won Detroit its "Murder City" tag. Scorched and gutted shells stood gaunt testimony to a revolution gone sour, decaying quietly under the glitzy veneer of Henry Ford Jr.'s Renaissance.

The last time I had had occasion to visit him, Moses True lived over a coin laundry in a two-story brickfront that had been three stories before some disgruntled minority type bought a Molotov cocktail for a window on the top floor. The building had that squat, startled look that such impromptu remodelings always leave. I walked past the closed laundry and mounted a steep rubber-runnered staircase leading up from the street door, which had a broken lock.

The second-story hallway, done over around the time of Hoover's inauguration, smelled of butts and old plaster. I didn't try to be quiet on my way down it, because the senile boards under the linoleum would have betrayed me anyway. True liked them that way; after the bars closed at 2:00 A.M. Sundays, he turned his place into a blind pig for the drinkers who didn't want to go home, and he preferred to hear the patter of big cop feet in plenty of time to hide the evidence.

The dogs started in the second I hit the landing. Dogs

were something else Moses True liked to have around. Big dogs, small dogs, dogs in between, young dogs in permanent heat, old dogs with one eye and no teeth. Noisy dogs mostly. He had been cited many times for keeping a kennel in the city, but so far there was no record of a True dollar ever having found its way into the treasury. The racket had my nerves doing headstands by the time I reached his door. I knocked before I had time to realize how unnecessary that was. The barking took on a frenzied pitch inside.

I gave my host a few minutes to step into his shorts, then knocked again. Claws scrabbled at the door. Some more minutes, and then I got my laminated investigator's photostat out of my wallet, twisted the doorknob away from the jamb, and worked the card between the latch and the strikeplate. It took me only twice as long to hear the snap as it does on television. I reached back under my coat and gripped my Smith & Wesson in its belt holster and opened the door a crack. A black muzzle and yellow fangs tried to force their way through to my leg. I fetched the snout a smart kick and its owner drew back, whining. I stepped inside quickly and leaned the door shut. A great slab of solid stink struck me full in the face.

Housebreaking animals was not one of True's specialties. The apartment, which was all one room taking up the entire floor with a row of sooty windows at the back, was an obstacle course of piled droppings and urine standing in puddles on a thin rug whose original color was debatable. Loose hair covered several unmatched chairs with burst cushions. Muddy paw prints bled down the refrigerator door and patterned the kitchen table's sheet-metal top. Shreds of linen that had once been white and flesh-colored foam rubber clung to the filth on the floor, evidence of a recent tug-of-war with a pillow. Everything was worse than I remembered it. His drinking customers had to be three-quarters gone before they came up there.

I shook off a white terrier that was trying to make love to my leg and slid along the wall to where a tattered curtain masked the bed and bath area, watching an eighty-pound brown Labrador retriever whose yellow eyes followed me from its crouch in the middle of the floor, accompanied by a long, bubbling growl. I had to step around something that looked like a cross between a rat and a Mexican hairless squatting to water the rug. A medium-sized mongrel with a square head and neutral coloring sat nearby watching me with a bored expression. I steadied the revolver and tore aside the curtain.

A naked girl with a mop of tight blond curls was sitting up in bed with her back pressed as close to the headboard as it could go without leaving a dent, staring at me with eyes like the fried eggs I hadn't had for breakfast. She was holding a sheet over her breasts, but I could see her ribs. She couldn't have weighed as much as the Lab, which was still revving its engine close by. Her chest fluttered. Next to her, sprawled on his stomach, almost as skinny and just as naked, lay a small man whose skin was a deep, even brown from his ragged natural to his heels, where the dusty pink soles of his feet started. The mattress quivered under his juicy, broken snoring. Moses True, the Terror of Twelfth Street.

A faded flannel shirt and soiled jeans that could have belonged to either sex were heaped on the floor next to the bed. Since they were on the girl's side I scooped them up and tossed them onto her lap. She started, letting go a whimper.

I realized then that I was still holding the gun and lowered it. "I'm not here to chill anybody." I spoke loudly to make myself heard over the barking. It had fallen off a little. The dogs were getting used to me, all except the brown Lab. I kept an eye on it. "I got business with Valentino here. Why don't you cruise down to the Renaissance Center and wait for the lunch trade."

"I ain't no whore," she said after a moment. Her Tennessee twang could cut glass.

"I was giving you the benefit of the doubt. Doll up. I'd turn my back, only I'd look silly with a knife in it."

She got dressed, wriggling into the still-buttoned shirt as if it were a pullover, put on one rundown track shoe, found its mate under the bed and put it on, and left without a coat. They build them tough down there. The dogs sniffed at her heels and let her pass. I listened to her footsteps in the hall and on the stairs and heard the street door slam. Then I got a good grip on the thin mattress True was smeared on and yanked. He rolled over completely and landed on his back on the floor. The room shook a little, not much. He didn't weigh but a hundred pounds dressed and carrying his wallet.

He awoke with a *woof*, looked around confusedly— and scrambled under the bed. I didn't think he was going for his teddy bear. When he came back up waving a nickel-plated .357 magnum I leaned across the bed and placed the muzzle of my .38 against his smooth forehead. I drew back the hammer just for effect.

"They'll love you at the morgue," I told him. "They won't have to undress you for the autopsy."

He was dirty but he wasn't dumb. He laid his revolver on the bed and raised his hands. He was kneeling on the floor. I straightened, still covering him but at more practical range. The muzzle left a pale circle on his forehead that filled in rapidly with brown pigment. His face was spade-shaped, falling away drastically to a point below high cheekbones and wide-set eyes under a broad brow. Recognition seeped into his eyes.

"Yeah," he drawled. "I know you."

"Amos Walker. We met when you were peddling goofdust on Putnam. Right across from Murray High. For shame. Girls too. One of them was the runaway I was looking for."

"Man, someone got to do something about them kids' complexions. She run away again?"

"Probably. They usually do. I'm looking for someone else. A man named Bud Broderick."

The big dog was still growling. I'd ceased paying attention. It was like its master, a lot of lip and no teeth.

"Don't know the dude," said True.

"No? I'm surprised Paula Royce never mentioned him."

He knew that name. His eyes jerked to the magnum

lying on the mattress, then back up to my face slyly. I pretended not to notice.

"I'm not on your case," I said. "I'm not a cop. Makes no difference to me who's pushing on Twelfth and in Grosse Pointe, because there'll always be someone pushing on Twelfth and in Grosse Pointe. I'm looking for a guy that knows a woman. She's on prescription drugs and you're supplying her. All I want's her address."

He went for the gun then and I flicked mine across his face. Just a short snap, but the sight carried away some flesh from the bridge of his nose. Blood came to the torn notch and rolled out the bottom. He squealed just like a woman, clapping both hands to his face.

"You're an easy read, Mose." I picked up the magnum. "Paula Royce. Where's she live?"

"Jump, Grog!"

I spun toward the snarling Lab, which was a mistake. Before I could check myself, the bored mongrel with a square head sprang a full six feet from a sitting position and fastened itself on my gun arm.

The beast was mostly jaws. It hung straight down from my arm, crushing it with all the enthusiasm of a Mexican wife grinding corn. My wrist went numb under the pressure. The dog made no noise at all except to suck air in through its wide moist nostrils. I felt the Smith & Wesson slipping from my fingers. True got up to catch it.

I juggled the magnum in my left hand until I was holding it by the barrel and started clubbing the dog's skull. It whimpered a little far back in its throat. I kept thumping. It panted some and its jaws began to relax.

It dropped, taking half my coat sleeve with it. While it was falling, I twirled the magnum frontier style and cocked it clumsily with my left thumb. The pusher held up, a small naked brown man frozen in mid-rise, knees bent, hands reaching for the gun in my other hand. Blood smeared his features.

In the middle of the room, the Labrador had sat down to lick a paw.

Gasping like a sprinter, I pulled one foot out from under the unconscious mongrel. It was leaking blood down the back of its neck and its tongue showed between brown fangs, but its chest was pumping. My right sleeve hung in ribbons. The skin wasn't broken so far as I could tell. I had held on to the .38, not that it was of any use with the arm dead. "What the hell is that?" I nudged the dog with a toe.

"Pit bull and something else. He was all pit bull, you still be wearing him." True licked his lips, glanced down at the animal and back up at me. The movement was strangely doglike. He'd been living with them too long. "If he's wasted—"

"Forget him. He's got a skull like a Prussian helmet. Where's Paula Royce?"

He used up some of the rotten air in the room without saying anything. I made one of those motions you make with a gun.

"You won't shoot me, man. You have half the neighborhood up your ass 'fore the echo."

I grinned. "You've been hanging around Grosse Pointe too much, Mose. Down here if they don't hear shots every hour or so they haul you downtown for disturbing the noise. Where is she?"

Still he hesitated. I frowned, feeling the circulation returning in pins and needles to my right arm. It was taking entirely too long to worm the address of one customer out of him. I tilted the magnum's blunt barrel toward his left kneecap and started squeezing. He saw my finger whiten on the trigger. He blurted out a number and the name of a street in Iroquois Heights.

I relaxed my finger without moving the gun. "That's across the county line. Since when do you deliver out that far?"

"Man, I got a lot of new customers out that way. That's how you build trade."

Beads of moisture glittered like diamond dust on his forehead. I elevated the barrel and let down the hammer gently. "Man," I mocked him, "I hope you're not jerking me around."

"They don't call me True for kicks." His hands went to his crotch. A modest man was Moses True, tra la. I watched him closely.

"Why so tight with the information, True? More customers you can always get."

He scratched himself absently. "Maybe you got me up on the wrong side of bed."

"Maybe. But you're not that hard of a guy. Who burned Johnny Ralph Dorchet?"

"Old news, Walker. Even the fuzz shook theirselves loose of that one finally."

The question didn't seem to have surprised him.

"Dorchet was working the Pointe," I said. "A minute and a half after the paramedics finished sponging him and his business partners off the walls of his place on Erskine, you were up there playing out his hand. You must've been picking law out of your back teeth for months.''

"Not like you think. I was inside for unpaid traffic fines the night Johnny and his bloods caught that cold.''

"Who blew the whistle, you?''

He skinned his lips back past black gums. "Just sour luck. I got stopped busting a light and they run me in on a bench warrant.''

"Sour like cherry ice cream. You didn't just step into Dorchet's platform heels without someone was holding the shoehorn. Who was it?''

"Just fillin' a vacuum, boss. Just fillin' a vacuum.''

I gave up. He was too playful for someone standing on the wrong end of a Colt with blood on his face. Muscle playful. I holstered the Smith and inspected my forearm. It was bruised black to the elbow, but I could work the fingers and no important bones appeared to be broken. Grog was coming to at my feet, twitching his legs and smacking his lips like an old man remembering a childhood meal in his sleep. I backed my way between animals toward the door. The Lab got up and growled. I nodded at it as I pulled the door open behind me. "He and Jaws ought to take their act out of town.''

"Hey! What about my piece?''

"Look for it at the next police auction.'' The door closing set the dogs off again.

On the sidewalk in front of the building I paused to suck in lungfuls of clear cold air, but I knew I'd have to take another shower and live a little before the stink went away. I drove with my left hand on the wheel, stopped at the first mailbox I came to, wiped off the shiny magnum, and dropped it down the chute. Short of delivering it in person that was the surest route to police headquarters, if the mailman was honest.

6

I STOOD UNDER SCALDING WATER FOR THE BEST PART
of an hour scrubbing off kennel smell until my skin
started to peel, then climbed into a fresh suit and overcoat and took off. My right arm mostly got in the way.
Since I couldn't write with it just yet, I made a mental
note on my way down the driveway to charge a new
wardrobe to expenses.

Iroquois Heights was the kind of place you wanted to
live in if you were in the forty percent bracket and you
didn't care which pies your local public servants had
their fingers in so long as they kept their campaign vol-
unteers off your doorstep and the neighbor's junkie kid
away from your stereo. It was one of those jut-jawed
little communities that advertised on television warning
lawbreakers to steer clear of the city, and at election
time they put teeth in it by raiding some giggle parlor
or other that was casting too big a shadow. There was
a newspaper, but it was part of a chain belonging to a
sometime political hopeful and its editors had stiff necks
from looking the other way. The streets were clean, the

homes were kept up, and every block had a young oak growing out of a box on the sidewalk. From the mayor to the cop on the corner you could buy the whole place for pocket change.

I cruised past the house, parked around the corner, and walked back. It was a one-story white frame with garage attached, nonfunctional shutters on the windows, and a fat cedar trimmed into a perfect cone on the front lawn. A six-year-old Jeep Cherokee was parked in the asphalt driveway. The front door wore an antique brass knocker older than the house. I used it. Lurching footsteps approached and Bud Broderick swung open the door.

"Yeah?"

I blinked. His face was flushed and a little puffy, but I recognized Sandy Broderick's eyes. Bud was my height but outweighed me by twenty pounds. At least fifteen pounds of it was baby fat. He was wearing an open-necked white shirt and brown polyester pants and black socks thrust into brown loafers. His tawny hair was rumpled and his breath would intoxicate a prowl-car cop's balloon. He swayed a little, trying to focus on my face.

I remembered myself finally and extended a card. "Frank Waxhouse, Michigan Consolidated Gas. Can I get a look at your meter?"

He spent some time deciding which card to read first. I was holding just the one. The entryway made an L behind his left shoulder so that I couldn't see what was inside. A television set murmured not far away.

"Who is it?" The voice calling from beyond the L was female and young.

"Gas man." He slung the answer over his shoulder without turning his head. He'd given up trying to make out what was on the card. I could just as well have shown him the one from the encyclopedia firm and used the same cover.

"That can't be," said the voice. "They read the meter last week."

Bud stiffened.

I backed away a step. "Wrong neighborhood. I guess somebody screwed up."

"I guess somebody did. Get in here." He moved his right hand clumsily and showed me the round blue empty eye of death. He'd been holding it behind the door and I'd been too busy wondering what champagne to buy out of his father's thousand dollars to notice. The gun shook a little. I hate it when they do that. He swiveled aside as if he were on hinges and I stepped in past him, hands raised. If a professional had done that I'd have elbowed him in the stomach and taken my chances on disarming him. But a pro wouldn't have done that, and amateurs are a blank order. He just might have let daylight through me because he didn't know I was kidding.

And maybe I wouldn't have done anything in any case, because nothing in this world is like standing in front of a gun in a drunk's unsteady hand.

He marched me down a brief hallway that broadened without doors into a clean pocket-size living room with too much furniture in it and a portable black-and-white TV tuned in to a soap opera. Behind me, Bud depended on both walls to keep his face off the floor. I looked at a small young woman in a sweatshirt and slacks standing with her back to a doorway opposite. She had dark

51

eyes and straight black hair with bangs to her eyebrows. Her features were dark, even, not made up. She was barefoot.

On the screen, Dr. Alan Drake was breaking the news to his brother's wife June in her hospital bed that she'd be back doing Sani-Flush commercials by February. The scene was being played better than the one I was living. I wondered who Bud had been expecting when he came to the door heeled.

"If that's Bud, you have to be Paula," I told the barefoot girl.

Something hard punched me in the lower back. Why do they always feel compelled to do that? "That leaves you," said Bud, "unless your name really is Waxhouse."

"It's Walker. I talk just as well when I'm not at gunpoint. Some say even better."

"I'll take your word for it. Who shent—sent—you and what for?"

Gun talk. They hear it on the teatime movie and think it's mandatory.

I said, "I'm a P.I. That's private investigator to you. Emphasis on private. No one sends me anywhere. I'm being paid to look for you by your father."

He breathed some air through his mouth noisily. "Try again. I haven't seen my father since I was a kid, outside of the tube." He poked me again. I was getting my fill of that.

"Maybe he has credentials or something." The girl spoke with a vague musical accent. You had to be concentrating to hear it. Hispanic, but not Puerto Rican or

Cuban, both common locally. The things you trouble yourself with when death comes looking.

I said, "I'd get them out if I thought the son of the dean of Detroit newsmen wouldn't shoot them out of my hand. By way of my kidneys."

"I'll get them." She stepped forward.

"Stay put!" Sudden panic edged Bud's tone. "I'll take care of it."

"My wallet's in my left inside pocket," I informed him. "I should warn you I'm ticklish."

"Grit your teeth." The gun rattled, as they will when you switch hands on them. Then his right hand reached around under my raised right arm and inside my jacket. I moved quickly.

I brought my right arm down, pinning his to my body, and pivoted left, throwing my left shoulder hard into his chest with all my weight behind it. A rush of hot, stale liquor breath singed my eyebrows. I came up with the same shoulder under his chin, shutting his jaws for him with a hollow clop, then released his arm to scoop the gun out of his left hand. It was a .32 revolver. He was off balance and falling, but just to help him on his way I delivered a short backhand chop to the big muscle on the side of his neck with the edge of my left hand. He folded like a broken puppet.

The choreography was good, but I'd forgotten one of the dancers. I was turning to take a bow when something swished and I exploded in a shower of hot sparks that swarmed and fell and died in darkness.

7

MARTHA SOUTHBY FROM EL DORADO, ARKANSAS, HAD the dining room set and the electric range and was going to get a chance at the vacation for two in Jamaica.

I lay for several minutes with my eyes shut tight against the light, wondering who Martha Southby might be at all and why her good fortune had come to my attention in the first place. Slowly, like a rock eroding, I came to the realization that I was listening to an afternoon game show on television. I cranked open my lids, rolled my eyes in the direction the sound was coming from, started to black out again, and rolled them the other way. I recognized the rug and the furniture. I was stretched out on the floor of Paula Royce's living room with a lump the size of a cocker spaniel over my right ear. I raised my sore arm to touch its sticky surface. White pain arced between my temples and a wave of nausea climbed my throat. I swallowed it. Groaned.

A thousand feet overhead, a face moved between me and the ceiling. I couldn't make it out for the clouds, but I recognized the sweatshirt and slacks under it. She was holding my gun loosely down at her side.

"Can you talk?"

Again I tried to place the accent. Mexico? Panama? I moved my tongue sluggishly from side to side in my mouth, working off the flab of disuse. "Did Dr. Drake find a cure for June yet?"

"What?"

"I guess you don't speak delirium. Don't pay any attention to me." I didn't try to get up. Many minutes spent watching ceilings had taught me that the muscles are the last to respond after a blow to the skull. "What'd you hit me with, the Kern block?"

"A brass ashtray." She giggled nervously, but she wasn't the giggling type and it went flat. "I don't even smoke. It belongs to the people I rent from. You've been out close to half an hour. I held a mirror to your lips once to make sure you were breathing."

"I'm glad I didn't wake up then. A thing like that could scare a fellow into a coma. Where's Bud?"

She moved her head. I followed the movement to where a pile of something lay snoring under a blanket on the rug across the entryway. I'd thought the noise was going on in my head.

She said, "I tried to move him but I can't. I guess he's sleeping it off. He'd been drinking."

"You couldn't prove it by me." I felt for my wallet. The pocket where I keep it was flatter than my ego. She noted the action.

"Don't worry, I didn't roll you. I'll give it back when you leave. I had to look for identification. It says you really are a private detective."

"Investigator," I corrected automatically.

"What's the difference?"

"In this state, your license. The state cops issue them and being cops they get burned when someone who is not a cop starts calling himself a detective. Semantics. I'm talking for therapy."

"Is it true you're working for Bud's father?"

I nodded, wished I hadn't. I laid palm to floor and pried myself into something that resembled a sitting position. My senses buzzed around like disturbed flies and settled slowly. I fumbled for my cigarettes, found the pack, then didn't feel like taking it out. Too heavy. "What's he afraid of?"

"Nothing," she said. "For himself, anyway. He's protecting me, he thinks. That's why he moved in here. That's what the heroes always do in that junk he reads."

"You need protecting?"

She smiled that smile girls smile. Enigmatic, they call it. I call it a low ache. I said, "I don't guess it's any of my business. I'm just the guy who got his brains spilled because you thought I was someone you needed protecting from too. I'm just the guy Moses True sicked his mutt on because an aggravated assault beef looked sweeter to him than your address in my notebook. The reason he had your address to begin with is someone smeared the man who probably had it before and gave True Grosse Pointe with this charming place as a bonus. Jump right in and stop me when I start making sense."

She sat on the floor next to me, folding her legs under her. She was still barefoot. Her face looked a little pale under the dark coloring. Her knuckles were white on my gun in her lap, but it wasn't pointing at me. That was a novelty. Her eyes probed mine. "Moses True couldn't have had this address. I never gave it to him."

I had recovered enough strength to winch out a Winston. I paused, watching her, then struck a match. "Yeah, I thought he was forking it to me when he said he delivered out here. He probably followed you some night after you made a score."

"Why would he do that."

It wasn't even a question, just one of those things you say when you think it's expected but you're too tired or disgusted to sell anyone on it. I tipped smoke back down my gullet and shook out the match. I looked around, found a heavy brass ashtray I'd met before on the floor nearby, righted it, and dropped the match into the bowl. Nothing like it to eat the time your brain spends warming up.

"I think you know why," I said. "When you feel like telling someone besides good old Bud, use this." I found one of my cards and stuck it out.

She took it carefully by the edges as if it were made of brittle glass. She read it, looked down, appeared to notice my gun in her hand for the first time, and gave it to me butt first. There is a certain way a person handles a gun that says she's handled guns before. I tucked the observation into my creaking mental card file for future reference. She said, "I took out the bullets. I'm sorry I had to hurt you. I didn't know."

"It doesn't hurt that much less when someone hits me who does." I stuck the Smith behind my hipbone. "Will you hit me again if I call Bud's father and tell him where he is?"

"I'll have to move anyway. Too many people know where I live."

I managed to miss the walls getting up. My skull boomed like a tin hut in a high wind. I filled it with smoke. "Got coffee?"

She nodded, looking up at me. "I don't have any made, though."

"Make some. Meanwhile I'll try getting Tarzan onto the sofa without a wrecker."

She smiled—a real one this time—and climbed to her feet before I could put out a hand to help her.

Bud wasn't any heavier than a drugged walrus. When I had everything on the sofa but his legs and one arm, I hurled my shrieking discs into the nearest armchair and dragged over one of those telephones with the dial built into a receiver that's about as easy to hold in one hand as a flagstone. Sandy Broderick's soundstage baritone answered after two rings. He listened, said, "Wait for me," and hung up in my face. Next I called Sharon Esterhazy to say her boy was safe and that Broderick would give her the details later. She wanted to know where Bud was. I repeated what I'd said, said goodbye, and did some hanging up of my own before she could press me further.

After a brief search, I found a bottle in the stereo cabinet with an inch of Bourbon in the bottom. I used it straight from the bottle and was waiting for the heat to crawl up my spine when Paula came in carrying a steaming white china mug. She saw the dead soldier in my hand and shrugged.

"I only keep liquor in the house for Bud," she said,

setting down the mug on the end table next to the sofa. "I never could get used to it."

"Just as well you didn't. That stuff doesn't go with pills." She stood rubbing her right hand up and down her left forearm absently. It was hard to tell what kind of shape she had under the bags she wore. "I'll bet you got that information from Bud's mother. She caught me on a bad day. I don't usually zonk out."

"Save it. I'm just the hired help." I picked up the mug. "Better bring the pot. It's for old Iron Liver there."

She left and came back with a glass pot three-quarters full of black liquid.

"Salt too," I said.

"You mean table salt?"

"As much as you have."

She had an unopened box of Morton's. I opened it, poured a thimbleful into the mug, and stirred it with a pencil from the end table. Together we sat Bud up and I held his nose and dumped the mixture down his throat, fixed another, and sent it after the first. He coughed, spluttered, struggled, pleaded in a gasping voice for me to stop.

"Get a bucket," I said to Paula. "If you don't have one handy, any good-size container will do. Don't trip over anything on the way."

I gave him time for air while she hurried out, then filled the mug again, doctored it with salt, and forced half the contents down him. Bud was making familiar urgent noises when she returned carrying a large copper-bottomed pan. I seized it and put it in his lap just as he bent forward. He gave back two cups for each one he'd drunk.

I grinned. " 'When it rains it pours.' "

When he was finished, I set the pan on the floor and mopped his lips with my handkerchief. Oh, the life of a private eye. Then I emptied the mug into the pan and filled it with fresh coffee. I lifted it to his lips.

"No," he gasped, turning his head away. "No more. Please."

"One more, without salt. You want it the way you got the others?"

He didn't. I helped him put his hands on the mug and tilt it. He sipped, lowered it, breathed, raised it, sipped. Again. His face was the color of old cheese.

"I've never seen him drunk before," said Paula. "He's been under a lot of pressure."

"The hell with him. My head hurts." I waited for the mug and set it to one side when it was empty. Bud sat with his elbows on his knees, massaging his face and hair with both hands. After a moment he stopped, looking at me through his fingers.

"Who are you?"

"The Bourbon fairy."

A car door slammed. Daddy was here.

I OPENED THE DOOR. BRODERICK, HANDS IN THE POCKets of a station-issue overcoat with a fur collar, glanced at me, then past me, his face registering impatience when his vision collided with the wall of the entryway. He looked at me again, harder. "What the hell happened to you?"

"It all started when I flunked my high school aptitude test." I stepped away from the door.

He opened his mouth again, then closed it with a minute shake of his platinum head. He swept past me and around the corner into the living room. I closed the door and followed. Story of my life.

His back was to me, so I missed his expression when he saw Paula entering opposite. By the time he turned back in my direction he had on his Six O'Clock News face. "Where is he?" It wasn't the smoothly modulated voice of the microphone and the telephone. It never is, in person.

"Dolling himself up in the toilet," I said. "He had help going in. This is—"

"I'm sure I know who she is." He flicked loose the buttons on his overcoat. Underneath was a brown blazer with the station's logo on the breast pocket. He hadn't been home long after doing the noon report when I'd called. I wondered if he ever did loosen his necktie.

I tried again. "You ought to talk to her, Mr. Broderick. She's the audience you want to reach with your reports on narcotics."

"Are you on staff at the station, Walker?"

"Excuse it, please." I somersaulted a cigarette back and forth across the back of my hand. "Just for a minute there I forgot I'm just the guy that shovels out the stalls."

His face softened, falling in on itself under the crisp snow cliff of his hair. "You know that's not what I meant."

"Yeah, I know. Don't pay me any attention. My head hurts."

"You've done an excellent job, finding my son in less than twenty-four hours. You've earned a bonus." He reached inside his blazer.

"*I* owe *you*, Mr. Broderick. Three days' fee, less the cost of a new suit and overcoat and some gasoline. I'll explain it all in my report. You'll get the balance back as soon as I see my wallet."

The girl started a little, then crossed to a low chest that was holding up a lamp and opened a drawer and came over carrying my wallet, brushing past Broderick without a word. Her hand was cold to the touch. I bummed a pen off her and opened the check compartment and started to write one out for six hundred dollars.

Broderick said, "You're just wasting a check. The money's yours from a grateful client. Give it to the policemen's fund if you like."

I tore the check sidewise and lengthwise and voided the counterfoil and put the pieces away in the wallet and the wallet away in my jacket. That dedicated I'm not.

We stood around looking at each other for a little. Then Bud came in from the bathroom. He'd washed up and combed his hair, but the flush was still on his cheeks. He leaned on the jamb and tried to look like he was not leaning. His eyes locked on his father's shirt collar. Their focus was still vague.

The newscaster moved his shoulders that way he had. "I'm sure you'll excuse my son and me while we talk." He was addressing a wall.

"I'm not so—" Paula fell silent. Father and son looked at her. She turned toward me, but I was busy trying to touch my nose with the end of my unlit cigarette. She went into the kitchen. I took a step in that direction.

"There's no reason for you to stay, Walker," said Broderick, not impolitely. "Your job here is finished. You must have other business that needs tending."

"Thanks. I'm on my lunch hour." I kept moving.

8

THE KITCHEN WAS BRIGHT AND VENTILATED AND BIG
enough to move around in without having to file a flight
plan to get from the stove to the refrigerator, as at the
Grissoms' in Grosse Pointe, and it looked and smelled
like a place where meals were cooked and occasionally
burned, not like an eighty-year-old wall sampler or an
exhibit at Tomorrowland. A blob of dried egg clung
brazenly to the top of the oven door. I burned some
tobacco with my back to a slightly discolored wall and
watched Paula walloping pots and pans around and wiping the counter with short, savage strokes like a fighter
jabbing the heavy bag. Blowing off steam the way only
unliberated women still know how. I said, "How come
you don't catch cold?"

She stopped strangling water out of her damp cloth
into the sink and looked back at me. "What?"

"Hopping around barefoot on cold linoleum. That's
begging for it this time of year, especially for someone
from a warm climate."

She finished wringing, draped the cloth over a plastic

towel bar, and tilted her hips back against the sink, wiping her hands off on her plain white apron. She had large dark eyes and hollows in her cheeks, as if she'd had her back teeth dragged out in pursuit of that lean hungry look. I didn't think girls did that anymore. "Who are you working for, Mr. Walker?"

It doesn't pay to show surprise too often in my work, but now and then I slide, especially when I don't know I'm working. She saw it and rearranged her features quickly.

"What I mean is," she said, "you must be a secret agent or something. Most people think I'm a native."

I did a little rearranging of my own. "It's not obvious. You pronounce some words a little too carefully for someone who grew up with the language. South America, right?"

She nodded quickly. "Bolivia. My parents brought me here when I was eight. My father was American, but he was raised in Chile. I spoke English in school and Spanish at home. I still tend to slip into it when I get mad, though not as much as I used to."

"Do your parents live around here?"

"They were killed five years ago in an auto accident. Don't say you're sorry. It was five years ago."

"I wasn't going to." I flipped my butt into the sink. It spat and died. "Iroquois Heights is a steep climb for an orphan from a poor country."

"I have an outside income. Are you being a detective or just a busybody?"

"How would you have me?"

Her smile was fleeting. "I think I would have you quiet."

"That's too tall an order. I like to talk." I found some dust on my knees and brushed it off. It was getting so I couldn't keep a suit clean anymore. "I guess he's got it pretty bad. Bud. Twenty-year-old boys who have lived at home all their lives don't turn their back on Mom's tuna casserole for just anything with long hair and a high voice."

"Bud's in love with the idea of independence, that's all. He just hasn't figured out yet that it won't last any longer than his savings. Also he has a hero complex like any other twenty-year-old boy who reads too much. He should go to school and prepare for a career. That's what I'd do if I had rich parents. And I doubt that his mother's cooked a meal since she married his stepfather."

"That's exactly what his mother said. About school, I mean. I can see why you and she don't get along. Did you want Bud to move in?"

"That's a very personal question," she said. "What makes you think I'd answer it?"

"Fern Esterhazy says it's my pretty brown eyes."

She laughed. The transformation was like emerging from a tunnel into bright sunlight. "I like Fern. She wants everyone to think she's a tramp, but she's a nice girl underneath."

"Underneath what?"

That dulled her amusement a little. She said, "I like you too, even though you're not as funny as you seem to think you are. I don't know if I wanted him to move in. I didn't not want him to. Or is that the same thing?"

"Not by a mile. I don't want to lug around a gun,

but there are times when I don't not want to, like every time I come to this town.''

"What's wrong with Iroquois Heights?"

"Let's see. The city prosecutor runs the town and he's a crook. The police department has several hundred thousand federal revenue-sharing dollars tied up in enough electronic flash to remake *Star Wars*, but what the cops get the most use out of is their twelve-volt cattle prods. Any Saturday night you can ring three longs and two shorts on some rich resident's doorbell and be shown into the basement where a dogfight is going on. There's a former city attorney named Stillson on the main drag who specializes in probate work, but if you're a friend of a friend and have twenty thousand to spare he'll make you the proud parent of a brand new black-market baby. If you're hot he'll sell you a complete new set of identification for a grand. What's wrong with Iroquois Heights? I'll tell you what's right with it. There isn't as much of it as there is of Detroit.''

Someone raised his voice in the living room. The wall shook. Glass crashed. I pushed through the swinging door a step ahead of the girl.

Papa Broderick was half-sitting on a pedestal table canted back against the wall on the other side of the television set. A black porcelain vase lay in six pieces on the floor at the foot of the table. Bud stood glaring at his father with his fists clenched. The newscaster straightened with exaggerated dignity, tugged at his jacket, and touched a handkerchief to his mouth. It came away stained.

"Damn it," he said, "I'm going on camera again in four hours. If my lip's swollen—"

"Say that again and I'll make sure of it!" Bud was seething.

"You're not doing a whole hell of a lot of good here, Mr. Broderick," I said. "Why don't you tell Miss Royce you're sorry for what you said about her and let's you and me take the air?"

His colorless eyes flicked from face to face and lighted on my forehead. "I don't owe her any apologies."

Bud glared at me. "How come you know so much about what he said?"

"You're a very fast young man with your fists and a gun when it comes to the girl. What's to know?" I was looking at Broderick. "Let's you and me take the air."

The newscaster handed Bud his editorial face, the one he reserved for crime and urban blight. He was against them. "You two deserve each other. Just don't ever call me and expect me to put up bail."

Having delivered this devastating blow he left us. Poor Sandy Broderick. His whole livelihood was balanced on a dial the size of a beer coaster.

I glanced at the TV. Lucy was trying to get Ricky to agree to move to a larger apartment and not having much luck. The laugh track was in hysterics. I found my hat and coat and turned to Bud.

"This won't take, but the windmill hasn't been built that I can pass up. The girl can take care of herself in spite of you, and maybe even in spite of me too, sterling defender of the weak and oppressed that I am. She's got your gun in her pocket if it came to that."

His eyes went to Paula, then to the bulge in the left leg of her slacks.

She said, "The gun's mine. It's registered to me."

"Who are you?" Bud demanded of me for the second time. I paused, considering. I had a joke for it this time too, but Broderick's exit had ruined me for snazzy curtain-closers. I said nothing and vanished into broad daylight on a puff of smoke and a sneeze.

Thinking that that was the end of it.

9

It rained on Christmas Eve as predicted.

I turned out the lights in my little tin office on West Grand River and watched it come down, streaking the thin frost on the window and making the lights of the city run. A close friend had presented me with a bottle of twenty-four-year-old Scotch for the holiday and I was quietly knocking the head off it with a glass I kept in the desk for emergencies. That close friend and I having the same name in common. I had bought it with that part of Sandy Broderick's thousand left after satisfying my landlord, Detroit Edison, Michigan Bell, and the ready-to-wear emporium I commissioned all my clothing from in Greektown, minus a bone to the savings account just to keep the service charges from eating it up. Not counting a routine credit check at courtesy rate for a medium-size agency I sometimes do business with on the East Coast, I hadn't worked in a week, not since leaving Paula Royce's place in Iroquois Heights. Nobody has any use for private heat at yuletide. Husbands ditch their mistresses to spend the holidays with their families, store employees stop chiseling the management under the watchful eye of goosed security, kids stay home to avoid missing out on the loot come Christmas morning. Business would pick up after the first of the year when everyone was fed up to the hairline with peace and good will, but for now I was the forgotten man. I sipped unblended whisky and watched the rain.

The world hit me over the head with my own telephone. I tipped down what was in the glass and hung the receiver on my ear. "Hudson Bay lighthouse. Gus speaking."

There was dead air on the other end, then: "You don't sound like any Gus I ever knew, and I knew a couple."

A woman's voice, middle-register but trying hard for husky. A shade alcoholic, but I didn't hold it against her, because I was a shade alcoholic myself. I said, "You sound like a Fern. Or do Ferns make sounds?"

"This one does. I tried to get you at your place. Don't you ever go home?"

"Every Leap Year Day, just to feed my four-year locust."

"What are you doing this festive eve?"

"Nothing I wouldn't rather be doing with Candace Bergen on the beach at St. Tropez."

She blew air. I could almost smell the smoke. "I'll call the airport. You know The Chord Progression on Livernois?"

I said I knew it. "Wear heels," she said, and broke the connection.

I hung up and drained my glass, staring into a dark

corner of the office. The rain was just water leaking out of the sky now that I knew I had to go out in it. I broke out the foul-weather gear and dangled.

ENTERING A JAZZ CLUB IN FULL STRIDE FROM A RAINY street is a little like walking around a corner into a fire fight. I stood in the dimly lit entrance a moment, stopped by a wall of amplified noise while a frat kid in plaid dinner jacket and black bow tie frowned over his reservation book at the puddle I was making on the paisley carpet. Someone was banging hell out of a piano in the cave beyond the lighted area, but I didn't hear any wood splintering yet so I figured the show was just getting started.

"We're full up, mister. Try us after New Year's." The frat kid had priced my suit and raincoat at a glance. His tone said he'd made that tonight in tips.

I told him I was meeting Fern Esterhazy. His expression thawed a little. "Uh, yes, she said she was meeting a gentleman. You'll find her at the bar." We were both men of the world now, his attitude implied, brothers of the eager thigh. I had a necktie older than he was.

I left my stuff at the window with an aging hatcheck girl and pried a path through the darkness and smoke hanging beyond the arch. The Chord Progression had started out topless under another name, but a previous administration had nickel-and-dimed it to death with citations for overcrowding and serving drinks to minors. The new owners had redecorated and advertised it as a place to hear topflight musicians of international renown. Instead, the slow, rolling death of the auto industry had made it a showcase for what passed as local talent. On the bandstand a black pianist with a weight-lifter's torso was tearing chords out of the keyboard in long, ragged strips while his partners on horn and bass stood by nodding and grunting behind dark glasses. It sounded to me like someone kicking a box of Lincoln Logs downstairs, but then I'm a Fats Waller man. Customers at tables visible in the glow of the baby spot seemed to be enjoying it. At six bucks for a glass of alcohol and fizz they'd better.

The Fern, in a shimmering green evening gown with a ninety-day neckline, was seated on a red stool at the bar arguing with a teenage bartender in a yellow jacket. Her voice was more nasal now.

"What are you, some kind of sex-changed Emily Post? Your job's to keep this glass full. When I want your opinion on how a lady should act I'll call you. Don't break any dates to wait by the phone."

The teenager touched his bow tie. "It's not my rule, ma'am. Management says no unescorted ladies at the bar. I stuck my neck out serving you two here already. I've only had this job a week and a half. I'd sort of like to hang on to it till I see my first paycheck."

"I know your boss, sonny."

"Yes, ma'am. So do I. What he says is no unescorted ladies at the bar and no unescorted ladies at the bar is what he says."

"She's escorted," I said, slipping onto the stool next to hers. "One more for the lady, and a glass of Scotch I can stand up in."

The bartender's face wore a thin sheet of suspicion. He had a coppery sprouting on his long upper lip that looked as if it had taken a month to show. He said, "You know her from somewhere, or this a pickup?"

Meaning was she wildcatting without kicking in to the house. I turned to her. "You left the cap off the toothpaste tube this morning."

She beckoned the bartender closer with her index finger. When he leaned his ear down: "Call a cop. I don't know this guy from Billy Graham's chauffeur."

Still hunched, he slid hostile eyes in my direction. Then they slid back to her face and he straightened. "Sure, green the help. I'm just trying to eat like everyone else." He moved off to fix the drinks.

"Class bars, phooey. Give me a dive down on Mt. Elliott anytime." She got out a cigarette and tapped it noisily atop the bar while she hunted in her purse for an Aqua-filter. Then she gave up and speared the weed between her lips cold.

I lit it and one for myself. "You've never been any closer to a Mt. Elliott dive than the Renaissance Club. I'm on to your act, remember?"

"You and everyone else. They all think I'm too good for me." She squirted smoke at the ceiling and looked at me. She had glitter-dust on her long eyelashes. Her thick red hair hung down her bare back to the stool. "Sorry I left you hanging before. I'm sensitive about my height."

The bartender brought our glasses and picked up the money I'd left him on the bar, made change from the cash register. I accepted it and stared at him until he moved down to the other end.

"Heard from Bud lately?" I asked Fern.

"He came by last night to drop off Christmas presents

for the family. Sharon asked him to stay but he said he had to get back. He's still living with Paula. How'd you find out where she lives?''

''I beat up a guy.''

She almost choked on her drink. She set it down and dabbed at the front of her dress with her droll cocktail napkin and killed the cigarette I'd just lit for her in a black ashtray mounded over with them on the bar. They all wore traces of her red lipstick. ''We're a good match,'' she said, squashing out the butt. ''We like to pretend we're hard. We're as hard as a couple of toasted marshmallows.''

''Philosophy yet,'' I said. ''Ain't we hell.''

She turned right around and took another one out of her pack. I let her fire this one up herself with a slim gold lighter from her purse. I had a hard enough time keeping up with my own bad habits. ''I hate this season,'' she said.

''So do I. Drink up and let's go caroling.''

''They start hyping it around Halloween and don't let up until it's time to start getting ready for the George Washington's Birthday sales. The air conditioners are still running in the stores while they're piping in 'Rudolph, the Red-Nose Reindeer.' ''

''Cute tune.''

''I bet all the bars in all the cities in the whole Christian world are jammed tonight.'' She ran a scarlet-nailed finger around the inside of her glass and tasted it. ''Chock full of toasted marshmallows like us busting their asses to make themselves merry. The hell with all of us. You can take all the mistletoe and all the trees and bright ribbons and shiny paper and cut-rate Santas and canned sleighbells and Perry Comos and sink them in the Detroit River with a rock. The last thing we need is a whole season just to remind us how alone we are.''

"You're right. Let's get married and be alone together.''

She smiled archly at our reflections in the mirror behind the bar. "You better watch it, brown eyes. I got rice in my bloodstream.''

"We'd last about a week.'' I put down what was in my glass and whistled through my teeth at the bartender. It irritated the hell out of him, which pleased Fern. "But it would be an interesting week.''

"It couldn't be any worse than the two tries I made. But I shouldn't fault them. I'm still collecting reparations from one husband.''

"What about the other?''

"He's in Jackson. We were together six weeks when he got himself busted for stealing a car. It wasn't his first beef and he's doing three to five.''

The bartender wet my glass. I paid him and he turned his back on us and went over to listen in on a conversation between two basketball fans three stools down. The good news from the bandstand was the pianist had finished his solo. The bad news was the horn player had started his. Fern watched me out the corner of her eye.

"I've moved out of the house,'' she said.

"Oh?''

"I've got an apartment off East Jeff, a little place. Four rooms, one and a half baths, and something called a kitchenette, but you wouldn't want to try to cook two eggs in it at the same time."

"Little place," I echoed. "What's Ford Auditorium, an efficiency apartment?"

"The husband I'm getting alimony from is on the board at GM. When he gets a raise, I get a raise."

"You said something about starving if you left home."

"I lied. Fact is I was too lazy to make the move. But there's no living with Sharon since she started blaming me for bringing Bud and Paula together."

I drained my glass. "Let's ditch the small talk and go straight to the seduction. My place or yours?"

She hesitated, then: "For shame. ERA and all. A woman's supposed to be able to call a man these days without him thinking she's on the make. Don't you ever watch TV?"

"Only when Sandy Broderick's on."

"That eunuch." She drank.

I wrinkled my brow. "Him too? You must have finished with the A's already."

"Says you. I was being the proper little hostess that day Sharon told him about Bud. He acted like I had rabies. I think he's afraid of sex."

"Who isn't?" I reached across her to grind out my stub. Something stroked the inside of my thigh lightly. When I glanced down, her hand was back in her own lap. She was toasting herself in the mirror.

The trio was jamming now, sleepwalking through something that sounded like "Lullaby of Birdland" if you closed your eyes, but only if you closed your ears too. Fern said, "I'm sick of this dump. Did you bring your car?"

"I think I left it in the parking lot."

She topped off the pile in the ashtray and picked up her purse. "Let's go riding somewhere."

"Somewhere like East Jeff?"

She grinned and got up, swaying a little, not too much.

10

I HELPED HER INTO A FUR COAT THAT WOULD HAVE kept me in gas and oil for a year and we left. Leaning on my arm, she slouched a bit to appear shorter than I in her two-inch heels. She was leaning a little too heavily for anyone within a yard of sober. There wasn't room for her between my lap and the steering wheel, so she just huddled close and rested her head on my shoulder. Female musk filled the car. I tooled north on Livernois and swung east onto Vernor, hydroplaning a little on the water standing on the pavement. Without a buzz on I'd probably have lost it right there. The rain had paused for breath, and in the glow of my headlamps the street shone as smooth and treacherous as a glass highway.

"Nice muscles." She was stroking my right arm. "How is it someone who pumps as much smoke and anesthetic into his system as you do feels like the Mighty Thor?"

"I get out and throw the hammer around every Ragnarok."

"You're full of surprises. Maybe we really should get married."

"Once did it for me. It's not at all like peanuts." I got my arm loose and turned on the heater. The fan pushed refrigerator air at my feet. New cars.

"Who killed Johnny Ralph Dorchet?" I asked, after we had gone a couple of blocks in silence.

"I thought it was Cock Robin." She stirred a little at my side. Her tone was sleepy.

"I figured maybe you'd heard something. It couldn't have been the local crowd. They'd have replaced him with someone who could handle Dorchet's racket without having to be told when to go to the bathroom and what to do when he got there. Anyone but Moses True."

She sat up, looking at me. Her face was taut in the light of a passing bar sign. "You are full of surprises."

"I thought you'd know True."

"Only by reputation. All bad. Why should I pay for pills when I get them free at parties?"

"Sometimes you might need a little something to get you from one to the next. I don't guess it's a disgrace anymore in your neighborhood. Maybe it never was. The air up there's too rare for a lug like me."

"You're a reverse snob, you know it?"

"I'm a dark-eyed Adonis who snaps women's hearts like breadsticks. Who killed Johnny Ralph?"

"I'd have to know he lived in the first place. I seem to have gotten along for twenty-six years not knowing." She slid low in the seat, resting the back of her head on top of it. It didn't make her look the least bit petite. "Was he a friend of yours?"

"I only know him by reputation," I said. "All bad."

"Then what's it to you who showed him the door?"

"I think Paula Royce knows. She isn't saying."

"Same question. Her account's paid, I heard. As far as you're concerned, anyway."

"Yeah." I whumped through an axle-deep puddle, spraying wings of muddy water up past the windows. The wipers came up once, shrugged some stray drops off the windshield, and went back to bed.

"I'll be damned," she said. "She did it again."

Her voice sounded strained. I looked at her, but I couldn't see her face for shadows. "I didn't know she did it before. Did what?"

"Did you just like she did Bud. How's she do it without apples?"

"You're snockered."

"And right. And sick. Stop the car."

I glanced at her again, then leaned into the curb, braked, and snapped on the dome light. Her face was gray-white and she was shivering. The rouge on her cheeks stood out like red wax.

"What were you drinking?" I asked.

"Gin and tonic." She smiled weakly. "Must've been the tonic."

"Can you hold out till your place?"

"I don't think so." The words came out in a string. She clawed open the door on the passenger's side.

I watched my reflection in the windshield, tinted green from the reflected dash light, and drummed my fingers on the steering wheel. I was spending a good deal of time lately listening to people throw up. The pay was lousy, but you couldn't beat the glamor.

She sagged back against the seat, breathing heavily. I gave her my handkerchief. She pressed it against her mouth and closed her eyes. The door on her side drifted almost shut. I reached across her lap and jerked it the rest of the way. "Going to live?"

She nodded with her eyes closed. "With my luck." It came from just in back of her tongue.

We resumed rolling. "Three drinks don't usually come down so heavy on you hardboiled types," I said. "That pill-and-alcohol combination's dynamite. It'll land you in a box one of these nights."

"I told you I only drop them at parties. I drank too fast, that's all." Her breath was coming more easily now. She tried to give me back my handkerchief. I told her to keep it.

The rain started up again, drumming the roof and stitching up the puddles standing in the street. Then it was over. I took the Edsel Ford to East Jefferson and turned down a private road lined with large brick houses, finally screwing the Olds into a space behind the one Fern pointed out. The lights of Windsor showed across the oily black surface of St. Clair. I unlocked the front door with her key and helped her, still wobbling on her stilts, up a broad staircase to the second floor. I used another key, found the wall switch, and stepped inside with her hanging on to my arm.

The living room was fifteen feet by ten with a brown-and-beige Oriental rug under a couple of modular sofas, a dark walnut table with curved legs and gold inlays all around the top, and a stereo console with a color TV screen hidden behind doors like a chamber pot. A casement window at the far end opened onto a wrought-iron balcony. A door to the left led into a room that was probably a study when it wasn't full of stacked cardboard cartons, and a hallway to the right gave access to two bedrooms and the aforementioned one and a half baths. Something that might have been called a kitchenette, containing the usual round of built-in cupboards and appliances and a square of red linoleum large enough for one person to stand on, jogged left just ahead of the balcony window. Light found its way in somehow through frosted panels in the ceilings. The apartment took up the whole floor.

When I finished the grand tour, I found Fern curled up at the end of one of the sofas. She had flung both her shoes in the general direction of the window. One of the straps that held up her gown had fallen down over a white shoulder from something less than neglect.

"Sorry I can't offer you coffee or anything corny like that," she said dreamily. "I'm still unpacking. There's a bottle of something in the kitchen cupboard, though, and glasses."

"We've both gone the distance with stuff that comes in bottles tonight." I dragged smoke down into my lungs. "You look a little green to me yet."

"I'm all right. Why don't you sit down over here?"

"Thanks, I've been sitting all night."

The raw silver in her eyes took on a hard glitter. "I guess my losing my lunch killed the mood. I do lots worse things. What do you want, Evening in Paris and candles?''

I took the Winston out of my mouth and looked at the end. "It doesn't happen very often," I said, "but every now and then in my work, someone gives me a horse. I just have to peek at its teeth. Odd considering my virile good looks and gorgeous build, but I still haven't come around to thinking of myself as the type a rich and attractive single lady would call up on Christmas Eve because she can't find a man to stack up against me. I ask myself, am I worth six hundred bucks in dress and two hours at the grooming station, and I have to answer no. Then I have to ask why me.''

"Could be I'm slumming.''

"Could be you are. I still have to ask why me.''

Her expression softened. She reclined slightly, and stretched a leg. The gown had a slit there that fell open to expose a rod and a half of silken thigh. "You're different, that's why you. You have wit—sort of. You don't mess with empty chatter, which is rare in my circle. And you don't believe it, but you are very good-looking, in the same way that a puma I saw once in the Detroit Zoo looked very good. Dangerous. I had a sudden craving for the exotic.''

I wrinkled my nose. "What do you mean, I have wit—sort of?''

She laughed and patted the sofa next to her hip. "Take a load off your brains.''

I finished my cigarette and went over and took a load off my brains. As I did I snatched a glimpse of myself in the casement window. *You good-looking puma, you.*

* * *

I GOT BACK ON THE ROAD AT 2:30 A.M. I DIDN'T MEET another car for miles. Colored lights hung in windows and on trees outside, casting elongated red and green reflections on the glossy street surface. The radio was playing "Silent Night." I started to sing along but forgot the words after "virgin mother and child." My mouth was dry. I thought of the bottle of good Scotch I'd left standing on my desk. The office was only a couple of miles out of my way. I shot past Hamtramck and home, got off the Ford onto Grand River, and double-parked in front of my building.

It's a three-story climb to where I do business at the end of an echoing hall decorated in early Warner Brothers. During the day I leave the door to the outer office unlocked so that any customers I might attract can sit down and read a period magazine while they wait. At night I lock it. I also turn out the light that was now spilling through the glass and across the hall. I had a visitor.

It was a hell of a time to be without a gun. I hadn't thought I'd need one to get a bottle out of my own office. I went back down to my car and returned carrying the Luger I kept in a special compartment under the dash. Avoiding loose boards under the runner, I crept along the edge of the hallway to the door with A. WALKER INVESTIGATIONS lettered in black on the pebbled glass and opened it noiselessly, inching the Luger and part of my face around the jamb.

Paula Royce was sitting on the upholstered bench looking straight at me. She was wearing a light blue belted vinyl raincoat and a soft felt hat like a man's with the brim pulled down all around her head. Her nostrils fluttered.

She had a gun I recognized in one hand.

11

SHE WAS CROWDED INTO THE FAR CORNER OF THE
bench, her free hand braced on the curved wooden arm,
the fingers spread and pressing so tight the bones showed
through the flesh. The .32 in her other hand—the same
gun I'd taken away from Bud a week earlier—was braced
on her knee and pointing where most of the muzzles in
this case had been pointing. It was too steady for a
frightened young woman from Bolivia. Her eyes were
very large under the pulled-down hat brim. The pupils
covered the irises. She was as high as a broadcast tower
and she didn't know me from Jack the Ripper.

I stood there holding my Luger and wondering how
long a man could live without breathing.

Time sneaked past, a great deal more of it than my
watch indicated later. Then her chin trembled and the
gun lay down on her leg, pulling her hand over with it.
My lungs started working again. I unclamped my fingers
from the jamb and came the rest of the way inside. It
was wonderful how I could do that without my feet
touching the floor. Lowering the automatic, I reached

down carefully with my other hand and slid the revolver out from under hers. It was that easy.

I sniffed the barrel. Spent cordite always smells the same. I rotated the cylinder, thumbing out shells and replacing them. Two empties. I dropped it into my coat pocket, there to pick up all kinds of interesting microscopic matter for the lab boys to scratch their heads over, and stuck the Luger inside my waistband.

"Let's you and me get cozy in the inner sanctum." I put out a hand.

She looked at it, as a pup will when you use it to try to direct her attention elsewhere, then reached up and grasped it. Her hand was cold as expected. I exerted very little pressure and she rose. I had to steer her toward the door marked PRIVATE, and while I was fumbling for the key she sagged against me with all her weight and I had to clamp my other arm around her to keep her face off my rug.

Not much to inventory in my brain studio. The same oak desk, too old to be smart and not old enough to be back in style, the same odd chairs and backless sofa, the same tired file cabinet with two drawers full of files, one full of cobwebs and mouse droppings, and a change of shirts in the fourth, the same green metal safe, the same framed original *Casablanca* poster mounted on the wall opposite my investigator's license in another frame and a peekaboo calendar to preserve the image. Dust and dead flies on the window sill. It was easier to catch leprechauns dancing on a sprig of heather than the building's fabled cleaning service at work. I deposited Paula in the customer's chair and walked around the desk and dropped into my swivel-shrieker still wearing my hat and coat.

This was yeoman labor, not fit for the expensive Scotch in the bottle on the desk. I swapped it for the pint of Hiram Walker's in the bottom drawer and poured myself a slug. That was my thinking brand. It went down in one easy installment.

"I'd offer you some," I said, "but I already did one lecture tonight about drugs and alcohol."

She made no response, but she'd heard me right enough. She was sitting on the edge of the chair with her knees pressed together and her hands in her lap like visitor's day at Miss Fremont's School for Genteel Young Ladies. Her back was unnaturally straight. I figured Benzedrine from the dilated pupils. Bennies and revolvers. Dr. Nitro, meet Mr. Glycerine.

I burned one cigarette, chain-lit another, and burned most of that. Not saying anything. Letting her get used to the place. There's something comfortingly clinical about two people sitting on either side of a desk that chases the dragons away. But not after three on a wet Christmas morning with two guns in the room, one of them fired very recently. Those two empty cartridges kept staring at me like hollow nightmare eyes. The tobacco had no taste. I made a face and mashed out the butt in my glass souvenir ashtray.

I started slow. "How'd you get in?"

She stirred, said, "I—I slipped the lock, like they do in the police shows, with my driver's license. It's not as easy as they make it look." Her voice was tight and very small, like a grown woman playing a little girl. The words tumbled out almost without pauses.

"Why here?"

"There was no place else. I didn't know where you lived. I was going to stay here tonight and wait for you to come in tomorrow morning."

"It's tomorrow now. Merry Christmas."

"Oh. I forgot."

I used the eraser end of a pencil to poke out a live ash in the tray. "I'm going to have to step pretty carefully here," I said. "There's a little matter of my license to practice and what I should and should not know to keep the cops happy and me in business. I want you just to answer the questions I ask and not volunteer anything. Am I coming through?" She nodded. "Tell me."

"I understand."

"Here we go, then. Where's Bud?"

"In the house in Iroquois Heights. In the kitchen. He—he's—"

"I asked where he is, not what he is. Don't volunteer. When did you leave?"

"I don't know. Eleven or twelve. I don't know. I didn't look at the clock. I just left."

"Where were you before you went into the kitchen and saw Bud?"

"In bed. I took some pills to sleep."

"That was when?"

"Around nine."

"Bud was in the house when you went to bed?"

"Yes. He was always in the house. He was afraid to leave me alone for more than an hour."

"Anyone else?"

"No."

I phrased the next one slowly, playing Russian roulette with words. "When you went to bed, before you woke up and went into the kitchen and saw Bud—how was he feeling?" Was he breathing, for instance.

She understood the question. "Very healthy."

So much for her role in the ballet. My throat opened up a little. "When you were in the bedroom, did you hear anything?"

"Maybe. I didn't think so when I—saw Bud. But I think now I heard a door slam. I thought that's what it was. I may have dreamed it. I can't tell you when I heard it; I'd been in bed for a while."

"Nothing else."

She shook her head quickly. Her eyes glistened. She was coming down from the uppers. Coming down hard enough to overshoot normal by a country mile. I had to work fast before I lost her.

"Let me bridge here. After you got up and saw Bud, you took something to open your eyes—a lot of some- things—and came straight to me. In what?"

"Bud's Jeep. My car was in the garage and his was blocking the driveway. I didn't want to waste time switching them around."

"You parked it where?"

"Around the corner on Stanley."

Right on my back porch. I knocked another inch off the bottle. The stuff burned a furrow like molten steel down my tobacco-roughened throat. "Back some. You found the gun in the kitchen?"

"In the living room, on the floor. I picked it up on my way through from the bedroom. That was before I found —"

"—time to get dressed. Brush your teeth. Gargle. Put on your false eyelashes and split."

"Yes." She spoke quietly, almost inaudibly. Her Spanish accent was thicker than normal. "Before I found time to do all that."

"I'm going to get hypothetical now. If something were to happen to good old Bud, if say he were to get his tongue caught in the car door and dragged to his reward, who would the cops figure did the driving?"

That threw her for a moment. She was dropping even faster than I'd feared. When you throw amphetamines up against barbiturates you just can't be sure who's going to win. "Me," she said finally. "They'd think it was me."

Well, I had to hear it. That was as far as I could take it without knocking over any of the pylons I'd set up for myself. "Are you ready to tell me what it was Bud thought he was protecting you from?"

"I can't." Large dark eyes, the pupils contracting even as I looked at them. She was having trouble closing her mouth now. It hung open between sentences. Blue-white teeth against dark skin. "It's not fair to get you involved."

"I'm involved. Lady, I'm involved. What do you want me to do?"

"I have to go someplace. Anyplace not here. I need time to think. I—I'm not sure I could face any kind of questioning just now. The people who would ask them have too many tricks." She got a hand inside a coat pocket on the second try, prowled around for a second, and came up with a key, which she dropped on the desk. "Bud's father—his stepfather, Esterhazy—has a cottage in Canada. He calls it his fishing cabin, although he doesn't fish. That's the only key. Bud said his stepfather gave it to him because he's too busy most of the time to get away and he thought a young man might like to be by himself from time to time. I imagine someone checked it out when Bud was missing. If I could just have a week alone I know I could face whatever's in store.''

"A week's forever in a homicide investigation. Hypothetically speaking." I studied the key without picking it up or touching it. That was the point of no return. "You want a chauffeur. The squeal would be out on your car and Bud's Jeep two minutes after someone wandered into your kitchen. Making me an accessory after the fact and probably half a dozen other nasty things the prosecutor's office will no doubt be able to dream up. Why am I doing this, again? I forgot."

By now her eyes were incapable of any kind of expression. "Maybe because you said a week ago you wanted to help."

"That wasn't meant to be a blank check."

"I'm just asking you to take me into Windsor. I'll catch a bus from there."

"Just down the block would hang me just as high." I got up and turned my back on her, looking out the window. Most of the colored lights were out now. The cityscape was this dark only once a year, when no early-morning cleaning crews were at work and parents were snatching dreams between stuffing stockings and that hour when the staircases rumbled under bare feet and greedy little hands tore the paper and ribbons off toys that grew steadily more expensive in relation to the dwindling time between reception and destruction. Somewhere on the east side a lone siren growled briefly and was silent. A routine traffic beef, or some bored uniform welcoming the holiday with a quick flip of the switch. No matter what time it is on what day, someone is always working somewhere.

I turned around and picked up the key. Why should I be any different?

12

The hallway on my floor had a brand new low-ered ceiling of pebbled glass panels. I took the custom-er's chair from the office and climbed up and raised one of the panels and ditched the .32 in the space between it and the old ceiling. It wouldn't still be there thirty minutes into a professional search, but it was the best I could do early on a Christmas morning.

I made the twelve-mile round trip in just under an hour. It can be done much faster, of course, but not with the prime suspect in a homicide in the car and every cop on wheels in the city on the prowl for early celebrants. I'd left my Luger in the office safe. Not long before, a group of visiting Baptist ministers had been arrested in the Detroit-Windsor Tunnel for carrying un-licensed firearms, and their pull was a lot greater than mine. My act added destroying evidence to the growing list of charges against me, but the weapon doesn't tell anyone much of anything when it belonged to the victim and has been handled by someone other than the per-petrator. Someone upon whom I was gambling an awful lot wasn't the perpetrator. Paula perked up as we left the Jeffries Freeway and wound onto Twenty-First Street, but she still wasn't talking.

"What about luggage?" I asked, when we were stopped for a light near the Ambassador Bridge. "Food?"

"I have money. I'll buy what I need. They have supermarkets and department stores there too. No one will look at me twice."

"Yeah, I bet they get a lot of Bolivians got up like Bette Davis." The light changed and we pulled away.

My quarters meant more to the toll guard than my face or my companion's. We hummed over the icy blackness of the Detroit River and stopped for Customs on the other side. A gray-uniformed Canuck with salt-and-pepper sideburns and kind eyes peered inside the car under the lights of the station and asked me my name and birthplace and why we were visiting Canada. I said we were seeing relatives. None of it meant anything, and he thanked me and said merry Christmas and promptly forgot about us. He would have said those same words to a hundred other drivers that night.

Windsor is just Detroit after the maid's been in. When we'd gone a couple of dozen blocks Paula had me pull over and she opened her door. The wind coming off the river sucked at the opening and spat grainy snow inside. They'd had some there, not enough to worry about. Farther north they put the parking meters on the sidewalk against the buildings so you can find them after they've had what they call a respectable snowfall, and they still don't worry about it. A sign in a lighted store window wished us happy holidays in French and English. She got a foot on the pavement and looked at me.

"I'll take the bus from here. I have a rough idea of the directions from hearing Bud talk about the cabin. Here." She held out a wad of cash taken from a coat pocket. She didn't carry a purse. "This is five hundred. I wish I could spare more."

I took it and gave her back half. "My day rate for escort duty," I said. "What are you going to tell the cops when they ask where you were and how you got there?"

"I hitched a ride."

"Guess again. When this breaks I'm going to the cops with hat in hand to tell them how I was duped into seeing you safely across the bridge."

"I was too far gone on pills to remember."

"That's no good either. If you were that mucked up you could have smoked Bud and not remember that the same way."

Her eyes were normal now, the pupils natural. "Maybe that's just what happened."

She got out and slammed the door and walked down the street and around the corner without looking back, holding down her hat with one hand. The wind snagged the hem of her raincoat. When she was out of sight I backed into an alley and went back the way I'd come.

I believed there was a fishing cabin the same way I believed she'd be back in a week to turn herself in.

I HIT THE SHEETS AT SIX AND JUST LAY THERE LISTENing to the antique clock in the living room bonging out the half hour and then the hour. But I must have dropped

off finally, because it seemed to strike eight only a minute later. Then someone leaned on the door buzzer the
way only one class of person in the whole world knows
how to lean on a door buzzer. I got up and threw on a
robe and shuffled to the front door in slippers while an
ache started behind my left eye and began the slow crawl
to the back of my skull.

"Amos Walker?"

I supported myself on the edge of the open door and
looked into a face that was mostly nose and a fistful of
teeth in a mouth that turned down at the corners when
it smiled, like a shark's. Its owner wore a long black
overcoat and a brown fur hat with a brim that dipped
down in front and a tuft of red feather stuck in the band.
He was my height, heavy in the shoulders. He looked
as if he could have taken me on the bright side of forty.
Probably he still could; as Paula had said, they've got
too many tricks. The other one, standing behind him
and a little to his left on my porch, was built slighter
than his companion and looked younger than I figured
he was. His features were regular and very black. Hatless, he had on a hip-length brown leather coat that hung
open over a jacket that didn't quite match his pants.
They were both wearing neckties. Most of them do, east
of the ABC wardrobe department.

I said, "Merry Christmas, officers."

The one with the nose and the downturned grin was
just getting out his ID and badge folder. He hesitated,
then put it away. "So you spotted us for heat, huh?
Maybe we should change deodorants."

"It wouldn't help."

He stopped smiling, but his teeth still showed. They

fascinated me. They were large and egg-shaped, and his lips couldn't cover them without looking as if he were trying to swallow an orange whole. "I'm Reuben Zorn, detective sergeant with the Iroquois Heights Police Department. That's my partner, Dick Bloodworth. We been trying to call you for an hour. What you been doing?"

"Stringing popcorn. I sleep hard. What's the beef?"

"The assistant chief wants to talk to you about the son of a client of yours that got himself a terminal headache last night or early this morning." He put an index finger to his temple and worked the thumb up and down twice.

"Which client is that?"

He told me. I didn't bother to act surprised. They look for that.

"I flunked current events in high school," I said. "What's the assistant chief up there calling himself these days?"

"Maybe you know him. He was an inspector down here till a year or so back. Name's Proust."

I sighed.

"He said some nice things about you, too." Zorn was grinning upside-down. "I'm off duty ten minutes now and the wife says if I miss another Christmas morning at home she's running off with a parole cop, so let's kind of shake a leg, huh?"

13

THE IROQUOIS HEIGHTS POLICE DEPARTMENT WORKED out of three floors in a fairly new building on the main drag, those floors linoleum-paved and washed in pale fluorescent light. The place was designed for breathing and elbow room, but cops had been using it for a while and that had had the usual effect. There were too many desks crammed into the detective bureau on the second floor, the stairwell reeked of stale tobacco, and the bulletin boards were elbow-deep in obsolete wanted circulars, two-month-old duty rosters, and newspaper cartoons as brown and brittle as last year's leaves. Disinfectant smell prowled the halls.

The place was as quiet as a hospital waiting room. A skeleton crew of uniforms and plainclothes men sat around slurping coffee out of Styrofoam cups and collecting double time for working the holiday. Over their feet on the desks and from the water cooler they watched Zorn, Bloodworth, and me as we paraded single-file along the wall to a door with ASSISTANT CHIEF MARK PROUST lettered in gold on the frosted glass. Next to the door, a two-foot aluminum Christmas tree shared a small library table with a Mr. Coffee machine, but in place of the usual ornaments, front-and-profile mug shots dangled from the branches. Police humor.

Zorn rapped once and we went into a small office with a gray carpet, the usual desk, file cabinet, and two chairs, no other furniture. The desk was just a desk holding up the usual desk stuff and a nameplate reading ASSISTANT CHIEF MARK PROUST. The plasterboard walls were hung with framed citations, one of those academy class pictures with rows of visored adolescents in sepia ovals, and a framed front page from the Iroquois Heights *Spectator* bearing a photograph of Proust shaking hands with the mayor under the headline MARK PROUST NAMED ASSISTANT CHIEF.

I figured I'd remember the name.

"Walker, Chief," said Zorn.

Proust took his time finishing the police report he was reading at his desk and looked up at me the way you look at a picture that needs straightening. His hair was more white than gray now, very thin at the temples from years spent rubbing against his old fedora, but his long face was the same, pale as paper pulp and sagging into jowls and deep pouches under his eyes. He was dressing better these days, in blue serge with a high shine and a gray-and-red-striped tie. When I knew him it was baggy gray wool and hand-painted nooses from the state fair.

He honored me for a long moment with his dishwater gaze. Then he smiled slowly with just his lowers. "Welcome to the suburbs, shamus. When was it we caught each other's act last? Wasn't it that time your old company commander got himself burned?"

"That's it," I said. "I bet the rubber hoses are lonely since you left the department."

"Always the card." He looked at Zorn. "You frisk him?"

The sergeant looked surprised. "You didn't say bring him in hard, Chief. He ain't under arrest."

"Yeah, right."

He made it sound like a temporary oversight. I wasn't packing anyway. My unregistered German meat-chopper was still in the safe in my office, and I'd left the Smith & Wesson locked in the desk. There was a gun or two lying around the house, but when cops issue an invitation it doesn't include your hardware.

Proust glanced down at my name on the report on his desk. In my work you learn to read upside-down. "You did a job a week ago for a party named Broderick?"

"You know that already," I said.

"You found his son here in town?"

"I didn't kill him."

"We didn't say you did. Yet. Sit down."

I was about to decline politely when the only other chair in the room was shoved against the back of my legs and Zorn's ham hand dropped to my shoulder and pushed me down onto the hard seat. Proust got up and strolled around the desk with his hands in his pants pockets. This was going to be interesting. He'd perfected his interrogation technique working for the old Detroit STRESS (Stop The Robberies, Enjoy Safe Streets) crackdown unit, the one dissolved by the present administration after the body count made national headlines.

"Christmas is a season for surprises," he began.

"It started with Mrs. Charles Esterhazy of Grosse Pointe, who decided to drop by one Paula Royce's place here in town about seven to wish her son the compliments of the holiday. She's booked a flight with her husband to Jamaica at eight-fifteen. The front door's locked and no one answers her knock, so she goes around back and tries the door there but it's locked too. So she peeks in through the kitchen window, and guess what she sees."

"Stockings hung by the mantel with care."

He went on as if I hadn't said anything. "She sees her son, one Bud Broderick, sprawled in his own brains on the kitchen floor. Her husband's waiting in the car and she runs screaming back to him. He gets on the horn to the mayor, who's a fellow member of his country club, gets him out of bed. The mayor turns around and gets the chief out of bed. Now, the chief don't like anyone else sleeping when he can't any more than the mayor, so he calls me, only he don't get me out of bed, he catches me opening a package with a necktie in it from my daughter-in-law. This one here." He waved the end of his red-and-gray tie. I'd thought it was a little quiet for him. He left it hanging outside his jacket. "I send Zorn and Bloodworth down to the Royce place and someone else over to talk to the boy's father, who just happens to be Sandy Broderick, the guy on the news. He don't shed a tear. He talks about the job you did for him and what happened at the Royce place a week ago. Then Zorn and Bloodworth get back and tell me they found this at the scene of the murder." He got one of my cards out of a pocket and showed it to me.

I shook a Winston out of my pack. "I might have

given it to her. I give a lot of them out. I can't be responsible for where they end up. What makes it murder? Gunshot wounds to the head are usually suicide.''

He leaned forward suddenly. His tie hung straight down like a tongue. "Who told you it was a gunshot wound? He could have had his head bashed in with a skillet. I didn't say anything about a gun.''

I pointed the cigarette at Zorn. "Your boy does a nice pantomime. Graphic.''

The sergeant shuffled under his superior's murderous scrutiny.

''You ought to tie a bell on your hounds if you don't know what they're doing," I told Proust.

"It's the entry,'' Bloodworth said.

Everyone stared at the black detective. Since I knew him they were the first words out of his mouth. He was playing with a loose thread on the seam of his leather coat sleeve and didn't catch his partner's warning signal.

He said, "Bullet entered under his chin and came out the top of his head. If they're going to do it that way they usually stick the gun in their mouth. Also there were no powder burns, so it wasn't even a contact wound. It reads like he was struggling with someone when it went off. Twice. Another bullet grazed his face, same angle. That could be just reflex, but like I said it doesn't read suicide on account of the entry and no powder burns. Oh, and did I mention the gun was missing? The gun was missing.''

Proust blew out his cheeks and pursed his lips, resembling a freshly landed carp. Zorn looked embarrassed, as if his partner had just spat on the rug. Cops have a thing about volunteering information, especially to a suspect. Bloodworth looked a little worried about the loose thread on his coat. Telling tales out of school wouldn't bother him, standing as he was on the solid gold of Affirmative Action. I was busy wondering if it was safe to start liking him.

The assistant chief jingled his keys in one pocket. For a space that was the only sound in the room. By the time he spoke he had scraped together enough poise to get by.

"Here's how we make it." He stopped jingling. "We know you had words with young Broderick last week from what his old man told us. He was a scrappy drunk. From what his mother told us before her doctor stuck her under sedation we also know the Royce broad's a doper. We found enough empty pill bottles on the premises to confirm that. Any pills she had on hand went with her when she smoked last night or early this morning. Lansing says she had a registered thirty-two revolver, and Bud was killed with a thirty-two. We're still looking for that. Bud got in an argument with her at the wrong time, when she was half gone on reds and Black Beauties and the rest of the rainbow. He was drunk; his body smells like the alley behind a ginmill and it's a sure bet his blood will test ninety proof at the lab. She got out the gun. They scuffled over it and it made noise, like Bloodworth said."

"Sounds plausible." I let smoke curl out from under my upper lip. "For something built on a piece of legal tissue in Lansing and a couple of empty bottles."

"There's a kid pushing life up in Marquette because of a partial thumbprint found in his uncle's basement.

What we can and can't build a case on depends on how many people want it out of sight and how bad. Mind telling us where you were last night between seven and midnight? The M.E. tells us Buddy boy ran out of breath somewhere in there.''

"I thought you had it tailored for the girl.''

He gave me his Lon Chaney Jr. smile, all bottom teeth. "I'm a civil servant. Humor me.''

"Rosecranz, the super in my building, can tell you I was in my office from about seven till nine. After that I was with Fern Esterhazy—that's Bud's stepsister—in The Chord Progression. The bartender there may remember me, though he won't want to. We went from there to her place in Grosse Pointe. I left there at two-thirty.''

Zorn leered. Proust pulled at his lower lip. "We'll talk to all of them. Then where'd you go?''

"Where does anyone go at two-thirty on a Christmas morning in Detroit?'' I asked. "Skinny-dipping in Lake St. Clair.''

"With or without the Esterhazy cunt?'' put in the sergeant.

"Shut up, shithead,'' Proust snapped. "We can do this smooth or we can do this rough, Walker. The book says we got to let you call a lawyer, but it don't say we can't show you the system first.''

"On what charge? I came up here voluntarily.''

"We forgot. Cops are human too.''

"Says you.''

His expression didn't change. He'd heard lots worse plenty of times. "Where were you from two-thirty until my men came to get you at eight?''

"In bed, like I told your boy Zorn."

We watched each other. Finally he said: "That's it?"

"I'm smart enough to come up with something better if it weren't true."

"I know you, Walker. You're dumb-smart. You're hoping that's just what we'll think."

I burned tobacco. Here was where I was going to bail out with my story about getting euchred into giving a suspected murderess a lift. If it had been anyone else but Proust asking the question I might have. I burned tobacco and said nothing. The assistant chief made brief eye contact with Zorn, who came away from the wall with his head down. His coat was open and he had his fur hat shoved back past a black widow's peak as sharp as a fish knife.

"We know what you was doing," he said. "You picked up the Royce cunt, or she picked you up, and you delivered her out of town, probably across the line in Ohio. Maybe Canada, but that's a sucker play and we don't figure you for that much of a sucker. That's why we found your card in front of the door where someone who's in a hurry might drop it on their way out. But like the chief said, us cops are human. We all got sour memories. Chances are we'll forget your name and what you look like once we got a line on the girl."

"You're missing Christmas morning, Sergeant," I said.

"Quit fucking around and read him his rights!" spat Proust.

"Charge?" Bloodworth had stopped fooling with the loose thread.

107

"We'll fill in that part later."

Zorn said, "Then can I check out, Chief? I'm working for free now an hour."

Proust wasn't listening. He was looking at the black detective. "You stay here, Officer. We'll talk about your loose gums and why you look at me like you just stepped in something everytime I give a simple order. Just because the mayor says I got to take you don't mean I got to take your crap."

"Okay." Bloodworth's jaw muscles twitched.

"Okay what, damn you?"

"Okay, Chief."

"Okay." He swung both barrels on me. "I'm not half as stupid as you think, Walker. No one could be. I know you're looking for headlines. 'Private Eye Refuses to Betray Client.' Pick up a little free advertising at the city's expense. Only it won't dry with me. I got an in with the local press and I can make you stink so high no client will come near you without a gas mask. That's if I get soft and don't bust your license in the meantime. Just try me if you don't—Yeah!" Someone had tapped at the door.

A skinny plainclothes man in shirtsleeves and a shoulder holster opened the door and leaned inside. "Silver Bells" trickled in from a radio in the squad room. "Prosecutor's here, Chief."

"You mean someone from his office?"

"No, it's the cheese himself."

"Christ, he must have radar." Proust stuck the end of his tie inside his jacket and did up the knot. "Okay, shoo the camera-happy bastard in."

The unidentified dick backed out. I remembered my

cigarette and knocked half an inch of ash off onto the rug. Making myself at home. Because if "prosecutor" meant who I suspected, the fun was just getting started.

14

CITY PROSECUTOR CECIL FISH STRODE IN AND STOPPED to look around as if wondering what the hell had happened to the trumpets he'd ordered. He was a smallish man in a neat brown three-piece suit under a trenchcoat and sporting a fresh carnation that on him looked like a sunflower. His graying blond hair was cut in youthful bangs, but the black-rimmed glasses he wore to mask the bags under his eyes put back every year the hairstyle took away. His expression said he was aware of that and he didn't like it one damn bit. He had pale blue eyes and a wart on one cheek painted black to resemble a mole. He looked ten years older and three inches shorter than he did on television.

I said before that you could buy Iroquois Heights for less than you'd stoop to pick up from the sidewalk, but you wouldn't get the prosecutor, not for that, not with a state senator's chair coming up empty next November. He couldn't see a thousand-dollar bill. A ten-grand campaign donation, however, would get you the key to the city and the promise of an appointment in Lansing after the swearing-in ceremony. He was famous both for raids on gambling halls and drug dens that made the front pages and for acquittals for lack of evidence that got buried among the obituaries. His kind is as American as Legionnaires' disease and twice as common. They can smell publicity from the downwind side of a stockyard.

Today he couldn't smell much of anything, because he had a cold. He reached into his jacket right past a crisp white handkerchief showing above the inside breast pocket and took out a Kleenex, into which he blew his slightly red nose with a delicate little honk. "This the suspect in the Broderick case?" His words were muffled by the tissue. He was looking straight at me.

Proust said, "He didn't do it, but we think he knows where the one who did is and helped her get there."

"What've you got on him?"

The assistant chief filled him in on the events of a week ago, mentioned my card and where it was found, and finished with my refusal to make a statement. I was beginning to feel like the guy who had wandered into his own funeral.

Fish tossed his wadded tissue into the wastebasket by the desk and came over and stood in front of me. "Your part in this is pretty transparent, mister," he said. "What've you got to say in your defense?"

I blew smoke in his face.

Bloodworth grinned suddenly, his bright teeth lighting up the room. Proust shot him a hard look, but met only grave respect.

"He's a hardcase, Cecil," snarled the assistant chief.

"He knows we don't have anything he couldn't slide out of with a little spit."

"Then we'll just have to make sure he doesn't spit." He turned to Proust. "I just got off the phone with Esterhazy. Maybe you never heard of him before today, but he draws a lot of water with the mayor and half the city council. Then there's the fact that this boy who was killed is the son of a popular Detroit television personality. I'm going to be shaking reporters off my lapels in a couple of hours. I sure hope you have something for me to tell them other than the usual dreck about all the leads you're following."

"I thought talking to the press about ongoing police investigations was my job." Something like color had come into the assistant chief's face.

"Not on something this big. Don't forget you only got this job because you kept the chief's nephew's name out of that drug raid you made on the Detroit school system. As a spokesman for this department you have all the media presence of a poisonous land snail."

Proust said something about which of them was more suited to fit inside a snail's shell and they were off. Bloodworth caught my eye and winked. I leaned over in my chair and whispered, "How long they been like this?"

"What time is it?"

Zorn, who had been consulting his wristwatch every ten seconds, took his partner literally. "Quarter after ten, for chrissake."

I twisted out what was left of my cigarette against a shoe sole and got up, flipping the butt at the wastebasket. "I'll just be on my way," I announced. "I won't even ask anyone to drive me back. I'll call a cab. That's my Christmas present to the taxpayers of Iroquois Heights.''

"You aren't going anywhere!"

Some of Fish's authority was lost in that he was shouting at my Adam's apple. I said, "Charge me or release me. You know the lyrics better than I do, or you should. I can hook a lawyer up here, but it's long distance and he'd just say the same thing anyway."

It got quiet enough in the office to hear "Winter Wonderland" playing on the other side of the door. I grasped the knob. Got that close.

The telephone on Proust's desk whirred. He picked up the receiver and barked his name into the mouthpiece. Then he listened, and as he listened his face subsided to its normal pasty color. He said, "Yeah," and hung up.

The prosecutor was looking at him, but as Proust turned away from the instrument his eyes went straight to Sergeant Zorn, standing next to the door. "He stays."

Zorn made a slight movement we both understood. I let go of the knob and moved away.

"That was Detroit," Proust told Fish. "I got out an APB on young Broderick's Jeep Cherokee when we couldn't turn it at Paula Royce's place. They just found it." He told him where.

Fish sucked his cheek, watching me. "Find him accommodations at County. Book him as a material witness for now, but show him the process. Whether we tack on accomplice after the fact and aiding and abetting is all up to you, Walker."

"Feed him his Miranda," Assistant Chief Mark Proust directed the sergeant.

THE COUNTY LOCKUP WAS A FOUR-STORY BRICK BOX squatting on a block of prime downtown real estate with a twelve-foot wall around the exercise yard and a narrow alley separating it from the Lawyers Building next door. It had been built back when criminals were punished instead of recycled, and although some reform-minded chief turnkey had had the plaster walls repainted a soothing turquoise, the tough old government green had begun to show through, bringing with it memories of leg irons and rubber truncheons and homosexual rapes in the shower room. Very little sunlight penetrated the iron mesh outside the windows to the corridors, lit day and night by fluorescent tubes and reeking of Lysol. The cells were medium gray all the time and had a dank stony smell, and a quieter place you will never see.

Zorn and Bloodworth ran me over after pictures and prints at the station and delivered me through a back door that led directly into the basement. A gray-haired guard signed for me there and took me to a brightly lit little room where a younger colleague sat reading a Michener novel at a yellow oak table with initials carved all over the top. For the next fifteen minutes they discussed last night's hockey game, taking time out from the play-by-play every few seconds to address me in the flat tones of men saying the same things they'd said a thousand times already. Empty the pockets. Leave them hanging inside out. Take off the tie. Take off the belt. Take out the shoelaces. Leave them on the table. Strip. Open your mouth wide. Spread your arms. Spread your legs. Turn around and face the wall. Bend your knees. Stoop. Get dressed. Hold on to that receipt for when you leave us. No receipt, no valuables.

"What, no stripes?"

Grayhead gave me the deadpan. "Funny, pal. Denims come after the prelim. That goalie couldn't catch a punch in the mouth if the coach caught him screwing his wife, Eddie. Later. Okay, comedian."

Out the door and a clanking elevator ride up to the second floor. The felony tank. Clackety-clack, clackety-clack down a waxed corridor to a cell two thirds of the way down. A couple of wolf-whistles from inmates along the way, but mostly no reaction at all. White-enameled bars worn down to dull steel where many hands had gripped them. Clang of the door, the guard's footsteps clacking away. Then silence.

My world measured eight feet by ten by my calculation, with a narrow creaking bunk bed and a lidless toilet that worked about as well as they do in most institutions, meaning unpredictably. By climbing up onto the top bunk and kneeling with the side of my face pressed against the barred window, I could just see through the thick glass and wire mesh to the handkerchief-size lot where the lawyers and judges parked their cars next door. It's not often you see that many Mercedes in one place. Directly under the window a pair of trustees were busy unloading a bread truck backed up to a dock opening off what was presumably the kitchen storeroom. No matter what time it is on what day, someone is always working somewhere.

I climbed back down and sat on the bottom bunk. I could feel the metal slats through the mattress, which was about as thick as a deck of cards and stuffed with cotton batting that was mostly bunched up toward the head end. At least I had the cell to myself. Cecil Fish's orders, most likely. Let the bastard stew for a while alone, make him desperate for someone to talk to, even if it's a cop. Everyone's a psychologist these days. Everyone didn't know me.

I wondered where Paula Royce was. I wondered who she was and what she was running from besides the law. I wondered who had handed Bud Broderick his ticket and why. I wondered what I was doing sitting all alone on a thin mattress in a quiet cell with a semifunctional toilet if I didn't know any of those other things. I wondered when they served supper. I hadn't eaten in close to twenty-four hours.

It was served at dusk, Monte Cristo style on a metal tray through a port in the bottom of the door, and consisted of some gray meat sliced paper-thin, powder and water pretending to be mashed potatoes under canned gravy, loose kernels of corn, a slice of bread, and a half-pint of milk in a cardboard carton. Plastic utensils. I consumed everything edible, using the bread to scoop the last of the gravy into my mouth. The food had an institutional flavor, but it filled all the empty spaces. Afterward I pushed the foul matter back out through the port for pickup as instructed by the trustee who had brought it, a harelip who walked with his right foot turned inward forty-five degrees. His shambling limp was distinguishable a hundred feet down the corridor. I would come to identify it with food and start salivating like Pavlov's dogs at the sound of it.

Dusk became evening, measured by a barely perceptible thickening of the shadows in the corners farthest from the light in the hall. Then interminable night. Writhing and stretching to burrow an acceptable configuration in the lumpy batting, finding it, then writhing and stretching again five seconds later. Staring at the slats in the bunk overhead. Doubts chasing thoughts through the dark abyss of the idle mind. No screams up there in felony, at least; those were all below in the drunk tank, where the inmates were wrestling with the furry purple things that came out when the buzz wore off, and on the top floor, which was a way-station before the upholstered rooms at Ypsilanti. Where I was was quiet. Backaches and doubts and quiet and the nagging nighttime fear of spending one's life in their company. The bland eternity of a night that didn't end until the morning shift came on to say it had. All for a promise no one much cared if I kept.

Happy holidays, Walker. Many more.

15

SOMEWHERE BETWEEN BREAKFAST AND LUNCH ON THE
second day, I was taken back down to the basement,
steered into a tiled room off the showers with a row of
sinks under a long streaked mirror, and handed a safety
razor and a can of shaving cream. I hadn't seen my
reflection in a while and it startled me. I looked like
every mug shot I'd ever seen. Under a guard's super-
vision I scraped off two days' stubble, washed my face,
combed my hair with my fingers—there was more gray
in it today—and I still looked like every mug shot I'd
ever seen.

"Why the spruce job?" I asked the turnkey, a young
deputy in the county uniform.

"I just take 'em where they tell me," he said. "I
don't ask how come."

I put on my shirt, gave back the razor and can, and
was escorted out; but instead of turning left toward the
elevator we bore right and followed the corridor into the
receiving area, where Zorn and Bloodworth were waiting.

"How's Mrs. Zorn?" I asked the sergeant. "Or did she run off with that parole cop?"

He wasn't smiling. "Back to the station, criminal. We got questions."

"New ones, I hope."

"You wish." He reached behind him under his coat and brought forth handcuffs. Bloodworth signed me out.

POLICE INTERROGATION ROOMS ARE NEITHER DESIGNED nor decorated. They just happen, like Dutch elm disease. Four blank walls set too close together around a table with a dozen cigarette burns in the top, a couple of hard chairs, butts in the dusty corners, that same stench of sweat and stale fear soaked deep into the walls. Nothing you couldn't pick out of a picture in the October 1945 issue of *Police Times*. The only thing missing was the heat lamp. In its place, an ordinary hundred-watt bulb protected by a steel cage in the ceiling shed even, medium-bright light into every corner. In a way that was worse, like the frank lighting in a morgue.

Zorn was the heavy. For an hour he pelted me with questions, now circling behind my chair so that I couldn't see what he was doing, now inserting his large nose before my face, spattering me with saliva, and giving me the full benefit of his nicotine breath. He kept coming back to Paula Royce; where was she? I grinned at him. He seized my collar in both fists and lifted me off the chair. Bloodworth pulled him away, said maybe he'd better go out for a cup of java. Zorn went out for a cup of java, slamming the door behind him hard enough to rattle the bulb in the ceiling.

The same tired routine.

Silence swelled the room on the sergeant's heels. I watched Bloodworth watching me, one foot planted on the seat of the other chair, arms folded on his raised knee, smoke dribbling out the end of a filtered Pall Mall between his brown fingers. Shirt cuffs turned back, spotted tie at half-mast. I said, "You the one that offers me a cigarette and calls me by my first name?"

He grunted, got his pack out of his shirt pocket, and tossed it to me. I slid one out and flipped back the rest.

"That wasn't really an act." He lit mine with a Zippo. "Rube is one cop who's as tough as he seems."

"I just came from a place where they pick their teeth with tough guys like him. They don't have to strut and make with the tight talk; they're the real thing."

"You caught him on a bad year. We all make allowances for Rube. He's got an eighteen-year-old wife that's making him crazy."

"I thought that was just a gag about the parole cop."

"The parole cop and just about everyone else on the department who is not named Dick Bloodworth." His grin came and went quickly. "Also it's this case. It's screwy."

"Screwy how?"

"Oh, the Royce girl's guilty, all right. One thing about this detective business is surface facts usually turn out to be everything they seem. Four years in plainclothes and I've never had a murder you could call a mystery. They're mostly open and shut. It's the girl's background giving us hell. She doesn't have one."

I sucked hard on the filter for taste and waited. After almost twenty-four hours without, it tasted enough like a Winston not to complain.

He said, "She was issued a Michigan driver's license sixteen months ago, which is about the time she registered the Buick Skylark we found in the garage. Her gun registration is dated a week later. According to her landlord she moved into the house that same week. No lease, but she got up first and last month's rent and a security deposit. Fifteen hundred. Cash. So he didn't bother to ask for references. Before that, nothing. She didn't exist."

"Probably an alias. What'd you get on her prints?"

"We're still waiting on Washington. Holidays. A set we lifted at the house matches what's on file with the gun permit in Lansing. It's obvious she was hiding from something. Could be when we find out from what we'll clear up somebody else's headache too." He lowered his eyelids, then raised them. "Proust would fry my ass if he knew I was telling you all this. But what the hell, he fries it whenever he gets the chance anyway."

"He was the same way down in D. Why do you think he stayed an inspector eight years?" I added some ash to the fine mulch on the floor. "So what's good old Rube squawking about?"

He found a scuff mark on the toe of the shoe he had propped up on the chair and rubbed it out with his fingers. "I'm not one to dump on his partner the minute his back's turned, but you know the River Rouge down by the Ford plant? Where the water's so warm from the chemicals you can boil an egg in it—only you wouldn't want to eat it afterwards? Sergeant Reuben Zorn's idea of a productive day involves sitting on the bank fishing that river."

"But you wouldn't want to dump on him the minute his back's turned," I said.

The quick bright grin again, like a light bulb blazing out.

I smoked up the room a little. "What kind of press is this drawing?"

"Turn to any channel any time of day and see if you can avoid Cecil Fish. So far you're an unidentified lead. About tomorrow, though, he'll have to release your name if he wants to stay on the front page. Unless, of course, we got it all wrapped up by then."

"Lots of luck, with that anchor they hung on you for a partner."

"Can that!" he said sharply. "You haven't spent two years with him, which is what buys me the right to talk about him like I do."

I canned it. I'd forgotten for a second he was a cop. Dangerous mistake.

The door opened and Zorn came in. He looked subdued, like a grass fire under control but still subject to sudden changes of wind. He glanced at Bloodworth, who shook his head almost imperceptibly.

"That's it for us for now, shamus," grumped the sergeant. "Fish wants his turn."

They handcuffed me again for the elevator trip up two floors to the prosecutor's office, where a three-man camera crew was busy rolling cable and packing equipment. Fish got up from behind a desk the size of a bed as we came in through the open door, but he hadn't seen us yet. He was talking to a slick number in a shiny gray suit, with one of those heads of curly brown hair that is almost always a wig.

"When did they say they need this tape?" The prosecutor peeled off his jacket.

"Next Tuesday. It's going into a sort of collage with that footage we shot of you speaking downtown and that pork-barrel session you had with those striking DPW workers last month. Servant of the people. It's corny as hell, but the voters expect some of that." The gray suit was flipping through papers attached to a clipboard in his hand.

"What's the rush? I won't be stumping till spring."

"Trust your old campaign manager. You want to go to bed with your public at night and wake up with them every morning right through to the first Tuesday in November."

Fish gave him that plastic grin you see a lot of around election time. "And all the while I'll be telling them it's the opposition that's screwing them."

Gray Suit spotted me, pulling a double take when he saw the cuffs. "Hold up," he said, laying a hand on the arm of the guy carrying the camera. "Cecil, a couple of minutes of you interrogating a prisoner would put some zip in that day-in-the-life gag. We can go dumb with it, use a voice-over."

"Keep that monkey organ out of my face or you'll be wearing it," I told the suit brightly.

Whether it was the cuffs or the wrinkled clothes or my Most Wanted look or a combination of all three, the blood slid out of his face.

"Forget it, Ed," said Fish, looking at me levelly. "That law-and-order stuff went out with George Wallace."

He steered his campaign manager to the door and gave

him a friendly but firm push with his hand on the other's back. The crew followed Ed out, glancing at me curiously as they passed. Fish's politician's smile lasted until the door was shut. Then he turned on Zorn.

"What's with the bracelets? Why not hang a neon sign on his ear, for chrissake? Don't the words 'secret witness' mean anything down on your floor?" His voice got high when he spoke rapidly.

Zorn unlocked the cuffs. "Department regs."

"More of Proust's bullshit, you mean. Wait outside."

The sergeant and Bloodworth went out. I rubbed my wrists. There's nothing quite like the bone-pinchers to remind you you're in confinement. Fish regarded me for a moment with his pale blue eyes, then strode past me, unbuttoning his shirtcuffs and turning them back as he went. He stepped through a side door and left it open. A moment later I heard water running.

The office was four times the size of my cell. The carpet was as green and spongy as the felt on a pool table, and bore the clear outlines of shoes and the marks made by the camera's casters. Squares of something that looked like real oak paneled the walls, set corner-to-corner checkerboard fashion with the grain going two ways. Sober brown law volumes stood in a tall bookcase against one wall, suitable for standing in front of when the cameras were turning. Opposite that a big square window with net curtains and venetian blinds framed downtown Iroquois Heights, and under the window were an ivory-colored sofa and a cocktail table for those in-depth interviews with women journalists with serious eyes and hurricane-proof coiffures. There wasn't a thing on the desk but a tape recorder and a telephone in a box like an infant's coffin.

So far I was just some more furniture where my host was concerned.

Fish came out of the bathroom buttoning his cuffs. His tie was done up and his face looked scrubbed and pink and a shade lighter than it had going in. The people we most hate and admire these days are all wearing make-up.

I said, "You'll never make state senator."

He started a little. His eyes narrowed behind the glasses. "Why do you say that?"

"Voters today like candidates who talk. That icy silence is strictly Calvin Coolidge."

He grunted and hooked his tailored jacket off the back of his desk chair. Putting it on: "I did some checking up on you."

"I get checked up on a lot. What did they say this time?"

"The exact wording doesn't matter. You're a smart operator. Not smart enough to stay on the sunny side of the authorities, but smart enough to make it good when you don't. Too smart anyhow to help a murderer escape justice."

"Then what am I doing counting cockroaches in the felony tank?"

"Because you're guilty as hell of being a smartass and smuggling out a suspect you think is innocent of the crime as charged. Your penchant for the white horse is public record; you've ridden it into more jams than you can count. But never as tight a one as this."

"On what evidence?" I said. "A business card

found at the scene of the shoot and a stolen Jeep parked around the corner from my office. You'd boot a rookie cop out of here if he came to you with a case like that.''

He smiled tightly, without showing teeth. ''Not if he had an eyewitness.''

My scalp started tingling.

''Even longtime private cops who know better can be taken in by appearances,'' he said, stroking the tape recorder on his desk. ''They think because the Customs officials on our side of the international border are ruder and ask sharper questions than the Canadians, they're the ones to look out for. But some of those geezers over there have good memories.''

I didn't say anything. Suddenly it was very cold in the office.

''We blew up Paula Royce's driver's license picture and yours from your investigator's photostat and circulated them among all the shifts on both ends of the tunnel and the bridge yesterday. A Simon LaFarge remembers checking you through the Ambassador in a late-model gray two-door around five Christmas morning. He's prepared to swear that a girl who looked like Paula Royce was riding with you.''

I smiled. I've done harder things, but not recently. ''Nice try, Fish. I bet you get a lot of confessions that way. From the guilty ones.''

''You did a dumb thing, Walker. Don't make it dumber. Twenty years dumber. That's the max for accomplice after the fact in this state.''

''That's *if* you arrest your chief suspect, *if* you can prove she pulled the trigger, and *if* this LaFarge character, if he exists, identifies her as the girl in the car. No statements for you today, counselor. I'll take my chances with the system.''

''Last chance,'' he said calmly. ''Talk into this machine and you walk out of here. No cuffs, no cops, nothing. Free as air. Otherwise we nail your ass to the flagpole.''

''Nuts to that. You're just looking for a big trial to grandstand your way into Lansing. I've done some things I won't admit to in this life, but helping hoist a showboater like you into a position where he can do some real harm over the body of a girl who was just standing in the wrong place at the wrong time in a wrong city won't be one of them. I'd like to go back to my nice quiet cell now. All this hobnobbing with cops and politicians is spoiling what's left of my good name.''

Fish's face was scarlet. He walked on stiff legs to the door and tore it open. Zorn and Bloodworth were loitering in the reception room. ''Tank this son of a bitch,'' snarled the prosecutor. To me: ''Get a lawyer. You're going to want someone to work on your appeal after we hang you.''

''Thanks. I've had my fill of them this trip.''

Zorn whistled on the way down in the elevator. He'd been eavesdropping.

I'D MISSED LUNCH, WHICH WAS NO ACCIDENT ON FISH'S part. Supper and night and breakfast again and the motionless lump of dead time in between. I had grown used to the mattress, and even the silence got so it didn't make my skin crawl anymore. Only forty-two hours inside and I was becoming institutionalized. One of the inmates in the cell next to mine, a lean young black with sideburns as wide as my hand, helped kill some of the hours asking and answering trivia questions about old movies. Fred Astaire musicals were his specialty. He was awaiting trial for raping and beating a seventy-year-old woman in her apartment and making off with a portable television set.

Sometime during the night, a kid busted for shoplifting tried to hang himself in his cell on the third floor and was cut down by a guard. We knew he was DOA at the emergency room of the local hospital before the jail administration did.

Footsteps in the hall at lunchtime, but not the scrape and shuffle of the trustee who brought the meals. They stopped outside my cell. I looked up from the bunk at the blue-chinned deputy who pulled the A.M. shift. He unlocked the door.

"Where's the priest?" I asked.

He said, "When you criminals going to get some new writers? Let's go."

He took me down to Receiving. The grayhead who had checked me in Christmas Day was standing behind his desk, upon which my overcoat was folded, the hat perched on top. He handed me a paper sack containing my wallet, keys, wristwatch, pad, and pencil, pushed a property slip across the desk, and held out a ballpoint pen. "Give me your copy of the original receipt and sign this. Make sure it's all there first."

I didn't move. "Who sprang me?"

"Authorization just came down from the city prosecutor's office." He wasn't going to say anything more. Then he did. "The Mounties fished a three-year-old Mustang out of Lake Ontario this morning. Your girlfriend was still in it."

16

"HEY, BEAUTIFUL HUNK."

I was standing on the sidewalk in front of the jail like an immigrant on Ellis Island, sucking free air and fingering a stale Winston out of my battered pack. Last night's snowfall had already melted off the street and been swept into yellow piles against the curb. Fern Esterhazy was sitting there behind the wheel of a green Jaguar with the top down. Her long red hair was windblown and she was wearing dark glasses and a leather coat with a standing collar.

I went over and said, "Crank the top up. The Ann-Margret look doesn't include blue skin."

"You ex-cons have no adventure in your souls. Hop in." I hopped in. The soft leather seat wrapped itself around me like an amorous stingray. "Let's just make circles till I can smell something besides Lysol."

We took off with a chirp of expensive rubber. I caught my hat and stuck it on the floor under the dash. The engine whined up the scale, gathering breath during the gear changes. She shifted like a Daytona veteran. I turned up my own collar against frostbite.

She said, "I tried to bail you out when I heard. They wouldn't let me."

"There's no bailing out a material witness. Who told you I was sprung?"

"Dad got a call from Cecil Fish this morning."

"What about Paula Royce?"

"Every time we meet you ask me the same thing. A Mountie spotted her last night driving a stolen car near Kingston and gave chase. They don't ride horses anymore, except in parades. She ran him around for a while, then went off a curve straight into the lake. She drowned."

"She wasn't that stupid."

"To steal a car, or to run it into the lake?"

"Both. Pull over a minute."

We were doing sixty through the business district. She down-shifted, braking at the same time, and we skidded into the curb. Gasoline romped around inside the tank. I pried my fingers loose from the padded dash, got out, and walked back a block to drop a quarter into a newspaper stand on the corner. A picture of Cecil Fish fielding questions at a press conference took up a fourth of the front page under a headline reading WITNESS HELD IN BRODERICK SLAYING. Below the fold was a smaller picture of me. I recognized it from my investigator's license photostat of two renewals ago. I paged through the paper, but there was nothing in it about the chase that had ended in Lake Ontario.

Fern appeared on foot beside me. "They just released the story," she said. "It won't be in print until tomorrow."

I stuck the paper under my arm. "How about a lift down to the police station?"

"Let go of it, Amos."

In broad daylight, her face showed faint lines like her stepmother's.

I said, "Just for a minute. I want to thank Assistant Chief Proust for his hospitality."

We went back to the car. She touched off a cigarette with the dash lighter and wheeled us into the traffic lane. "Bud was a sweet kid. I never thought I'd miss him but I do."

"You think the girl killed him?"

"I don't hate her for it. I wouldn't if she were still alive. It's not as if she planned it, or as if she knew what she was doing. You'd think she did it too, if you weren't still gone on her."

"I don't know that I've ever been gone on anyone," I said, "and neither do you. It's more complicated than that. I'd buy the police version of what happened—maybe—if I wasn't sure she was looking back over her shoulder all the time she was here. I want to know who it was she expected to see."

"Maybe it was herself. God, I'm Freudian today." She raised her cigarette above the windshield and tapped ash off into the slipstream. "I was in analysis, you know. Two years."

"Who wasn't, in your tax bracket? There's the cophouse. Dump me here. I'll walk across."

I had a hand on the door handle when she spun the Jag into a tight U and we shrieked to a halt in front of the steps leading up to the front door. When the shocks were through squeaking I picked my hat up off the floor and stepped up onto the curb. I resisted the urge to get down and kiss the concrete.

"How long will you be?" she asked.

"As long as it takes my knees to stop wobbling."

She smiled beatifically. "I'll be here when they do."

On my way up the steps I met a uniformed officer coming down. His cop's eyes flicked from the car to me and he said, "That's police parking only. Who's she, the Pope in drag?"

"Close. She's Charles Esterhazy's daughter."

His face got tired. He knew the name. "That figures. In this town everybody's somebody's."

Inside, the bald desk sergeant spotted me heading up the stairs and called out. I pretended not to hear. But he must have made a call to the squad room, because by the time I reached the second floor a detective was waiting for me. It was the same plainclothes man who had poked his head into Proust's office to announce the city prosecutor's arrival—was that only two days earlier? My life had fallen into two parts, before the slam and after.

I said, "Chief in?"

"Not to you, Jim." He was a thin twist of hide with a pockmarked face and an obvious Adam's apple that cleared his collar with three inches to spare. The strap of his underarm holster defied gravity clinging to his almost nonexistent shoulders. "No civilians above the street without an accompanying officer."

"I didn't see the X-rating downstairs."

"Look for it on your way out."

"Let the son of a bitch pass, Epstein."

At the guttural command, the detective glanced back at Proust leaning out through his office door, then moved just enough so that I had to walk around him to enter the squad room. The assistant chief held the door for me as I went into the office. I hear they do that for you in the gas chamber too.

He closed the door. "Seat."

"No thanks. My keister's still flat from that two-by-four in the icehouse."

"Suit yourself. How's county food these days?"

"They got food?"

He snickered and circled behind his desk, walking with a jaunty step. Same well-cut blue suit, but today he was wearing a maroon silk tie with a musical clef embroidered in gold just below the knot. I didn't know he'd been a musician.

"You got angels on your shoulder, Walker. If we'd latched on to Paula Royce anything but dead, the grand jury would've indicted you along with her for complicity. We could still hook you for withholding information in a felony case, but why bother? There's no percentage in holding a grudge."

I waited for the kicker. He lowered himself into his swivel chair with a pleasant little sigh and cracked a weary humidor on his desk to look over the cigars inside like a prom queen choosing from an assortment of chocolates. Then he sighed again, a little less contentedly, and flipped shut the lid without taking one. He was in too good a mood for someone who had just surrendered a plum to the Canadian authorities and was cutting down his tobacco consumption in the bargain. And he could hold a grudge till it sprouted leaves.

"You'll find a letter from state police headquarters in Lansing waiting for you at your office." His muddy eyes looked dreamy. "I called them yesterday early. They've yanked your license on charges lodged by this office."

"I can petition for a hearing," I said after a moment.

"Sure, but why mess around with it? You're guilty. I guess they'll be sending someone around to collect your plastic badge. You better give it to him. You know how hot those boys in the Hollywood Division get when they have to come get you and lose the crease in their pants."

"All that means is I can't do what I do and get paid. I've had plenty of practice at that."

He smiled, with both sets this time. "Everybody needs a hobby. Oh, and they're pulling your CCW too, so don't go around packing anything more lethal than a rubber in your wallet. I'm big on gun control."

"Yeah, I heard about your Howitzer collection." I scratched a match on the edge of his desk just to kick the smile off his face. It wasn't worth it. It had been done before. "What about the Broderick kill?"

"What about it?"

I hesitated before setting flame to tobacco. "That's how it is, huh."

"That's how it is. In this department we don't waste time sucking bare bones."

"Who ID'd Paula Royce's body?"

"Us. She fit the APB reader, so the moose patrol took her prints and telexed us a copy. Confirmed."

"Who'd you send up for the eyeball?"

"Prints is prints, citizen. We got to save on gasoline for the President." He unwound the string from a large manila envelope full of traffic accident reports and started reading. "Walk, now. You're in my light."

I used the door. When a cop tells you to walk you walk.

FERN WAS STILL PARKED IN THE *VERBOTEN* ZONE IN front of the station. As I approached, a young motor-cycle officer encased in glistening black leather from collar to toes turned away from the car and passed me, humming. He didn't have his ticket book out. His fat Harley was standing between the Jag and a gold Chrysler LeBaron in the first of the metered spaces behind.

"You must be sitting upwind of the kennel today." I climbed in beside Fern.

She studied me through her cheaters. "I heard prison is embittering. I didn't know it worked so fast."

"You're right. Sorry. Did I interrupt you and Brando while you were setting the date?"

"No chance. Too young and poor."

I tilted my hat forward over my eyes and rested the back of my head against the seat. "Drive, Kato."

"Where to?"

"The nearest office of the Michigan Employment Security Commission."

"Welfare cheat." She let out the clutch.

My eyes burned behind my lids. I was bled out, but I didn't sleep right away. My head was too full of why no one had gone to Canada to finger Paula Royce's remains, in a racket that demands two witnesses' signatures to requisition a roll of toilet paper.

I DREAMED I WAS BACK IN JAIL, TRYING TO SHUT OUT the clanging of barred doors reverberating through my cell. The hard bunk beneath me jumped with each impact. I opened my eyes. Fern Esterhazy's Jaguar was bucking over a series of traffic bumps in a residential neighborhood I knew well.

"Slow down," I said, sitting up. "That's what those things are for."

She eased back on the accelerator. I hooked out my pack, but it was empty. She offered me one of hers. I shook my head. My throat was still getting used to them. "How'd you find out where I live?"

"You're in the book, remember? My place was closer, but you need a shave and I don't have a razor. Whiskers are like snow scenes, nice to look at but not to feel."

"Unless my body is the price of the ride"—I yawned—"I'll just pass for now. All I'm hot for at the moment is sleep." I adjusted her mirror to monitor the growth on my chin. The gold Chrysler LeBaron reflected over my shoulder looked significant. I tried to remember why. Then I remembered. "Make a right," I said.

"This is your street."

"Make it anyway. While you're at it, make three more." She understood then and glanced at her side mirror. We circled the block.

"He's gone," she said, checking the mirror. Her tone was relieved.

"Yeah."

He was bright, but not bright enough. He'd left us after two turns. If he'd been wide awake he'd have dropped us after the first. I readjusted the mirror and settled back for the rest of the ride. So far I hadn't noticed much difference between the life of a private citizen and that of an investigator.

17

My chauffeur let me out at my house without a word and took off in a full-throated roar of burning money. I'd disappointed her by needing rest, it seemed. Lately I'd disappointed everyone but Assistant Chief Mark Proust. He loved me.

The air in the shack was stale. I left the front door open to let it exhale and mined a bottle of beer out of the refrigerator. It tasted of jail. I poured the rest of it down the sink and went into the living room and sat down in front of the TV set without turning it on. When I'd had enough of that I called my answering service for messages. There were four. One was from a woman whose mother had walked away from her nursing home Christmas Eve and hadn't been heard from since. One was from a place that wanted to sell me office furniture. Another was from a man named Horn who had tried to reach me that morning and said he'd try again later. The fourth was from the woman, canceling her earlier call. Her mother had been found and returned to the home.

I walked through the house slowly, but there were no

signs that the cops had frisked the place. The dust was undisturbed on the half-case of nine-millimeter Luger ammunition on the shelf of the bedroom closet, courtesy of a dealer who didn't share his colleagues' fetish for official paperwork. When you own an unlicensed weapon you try not to leave tracks leading to it.

I found the outcounty telephone directory and dialed the Iroquois Heights Police Department. I asked for Dick Bloodworth.

"He's gone for the day," said the voice I got. "This is Sergeant Dingle. Something I can do you for?"

"It's Bloodworth I want. What's his home number?"

"Sorry, we can't give that out."

"This is Deputy Wedge, armorer for the Wayne County Sheriff's Department. I just finished fitting a new grip to his side arm and I want to tell him he can pick it up."

"I'll call him and tell him."

Cops. I gave him my number to give to Bloodworth and we stopped talking to each other.

The telephone rang while I was peeling off my shirt.

"I'm looking at my side arm right now," Bloodworth's voice informed me. "Grip's the same one I been using since I got out of uniform. And how come I went across the line to Wayne County when we got an armorer of our own?"

I said, "I didn't know his name, and for all I knew it was him I was talking to. This is Walker. Remember me? I was wearing iron last time we spoke."

"Uh-huh." He waited.

"Listen, I want to talk to you about the Royce case."

"What Royce case? Ain't no Royce case, man. It's deader'n she is."

He'd gone dialect on me, a healthy sign for my purposes. "Trade you a sympathetic ear for some information."

"You'll be getting the short end," he said after a pause.

"There's another kind? Where can we meet?"

"My dump." He gave me an address in Iroquois Heights. "Make it at three. Right now I got to go out and shop for a new propeller." Click.

That one kept me awake for all of five minutes.

DICK BLOODWORTH LIVED IN A BRICK SPLIT-LEVEL IN one of the older subdivisions north of the city proper, with a big picture window and a low hedge and a basketball hoop mounted over the garage door. An iron jockey stood on the porch. Someone had slapped a coat of white paint over its black face and hands. That tattered old racial joke.

Mrs. Bloodworth greeted me cordially in a bulky turtleneck sweater and tight slacks over everything Fern Esterhazy had, only in a more compact package. Her complexion was a smooth *café au lait* and her hair was sprayed into glossy black waves as hard as corrugated steel. She hung my hat and coat in the hall closet and showed me an open door across the entryway with steps leading down from it.

"Dick's in the basement," she said. "Just follow the smell of glue."

The basement was carpeted and paneled. An oil furnace cut in with a click and a rush as I approached a

140

lighted doorway from which crawled a sharp stench of acetate. I was showered and shaved and wearing fresh clothes. I felt like an ex-con checking in with his parole officer.

"Second," Bloodworth said.

The room was small, paneled like the rest of the cellar and illuminated by two pairs of fluorescent tubes suspended from the ceiling in troughs. Model airplanes of every size, type, period, and color hung from wires and perched on tables and benches and steel utility shelves all over the room, so close together you needed a diagram to cross the floor without bumping into any. The detective was hunched over a British Spitfire with a fuselage as long as a man's leg clamped in a vise on a plain wooden bench, hooking a wire across from a dry-cell battery to a terminal on a tiny electric motor in the nose. Straightening, he picked up a remote control device, pointed the antenna at the motor, and flipped a switch. The propeller spun with a sputtering noise that quickly became a drone. He flipped the switch back the other way and it coughed to a stop.

"So this is what you cops do with your spare time," I said. "Another mystery solved."

He put down the remote control and wiped his hands off on a smeared cotton rag. He was dressed in a white T-shirt and soiled jeans. Muscles leaped and twitched in his arms and chest as he kneaded the rag. "Depends on the cop. Some drink, some whore around. I play with toys. Keeps my mind off the drinks and the whores. There's brew in the refrigerator. Toss me a can and grab one for yourself."

A camp-size unit occupied the corner behind the open

door. I got out two cans and handed him one, zipping the top off mine. It was starting to taste like beer again. He took a seat on a round stool next to the bench and waved me into a comfortable shabby overstuffed chair under a dogfight between a squadron of Fokkers and a French Spad, frozen in time and space like moths in a light fixture. I peeled the cellophane off a fresh pack and lit up and drank beer and smoked and watched him.

"My fly open?" he asked after a minute.

"I was just exercising my noggin. You strike me as reasonably honest."

He slipped into dialect. "Some of us is, boss."

"Cut that crap. You've got too much going for you to hide behind pigment. How's a reasonably honest guy wind up packing a star in a place like Iroquois Heights?"

"You don't know that I'm honest," he said, "reasonably or otherwise."

"You have to be. If you weren't, times being what times are, you wouldn't still be holding doors for deadwood like Reuben Zorn after four years in plainclothes. You'd be Cecil Fish's chief investigator, or something else equally visible. My guess is you're too dangerous even for window-dressing, which in this town means straight—reasonably speaking."

He bolted the contents of his can and flipped it into a wastebasket stuffed full of glue-streaked newspaper. Some beer-drinkers are like that. "So what's the pitch?"

"Who slammed the door on the Broderick shoot and why so fast?"

"I don't know."

"You don't know who, or you don't know why?"

"I don't know means I don't know. All I do know is

142

Rube and I were busy jacking up the neighbors for the inside track on Paula Royce when we got the call-back to the station. Twenty minutes later we're turning a B-and-E at a drugstore downtown. The Royce girl was dead and it was all over but the paperwork, and there wasn't even as much of that as we're used to.''

"What'd you get from the neighbors?''

"The big O, just like we got from Washington on her prints. No one on the block even knew her name before the story broke. We got eighteen months out of twenty-four years, and we don't even have that, really. Where was she before she moved here? Where'd her money come from? She didn't work, and young Broderick barely had enough in his savings account to support himself if he stayed low, let alone the two of them. I don't think I like mysteries. If I did I wouldn't have become a detective.''

He unrolled a pack and a book of matches from his T-shirt sleeve. While he was lighting up I said, "She told me she was from Bolivia. Her parents were—'' I stopped.

He looked at me until the match burned down to his fingers, then dropped it and ground it out under his heel on the carpet. "Yeah?''

I leaned down carefully, tipped some ash into my pantcuff, and sat back. "Her parents were both killed in an automobile accident, or so she claimed. With what happened to her that's two in one family. What are the odds on something like that?''

"I'd say pretty good. There are a lot of cars in the world.''

"Maybe." I sucked smoke. "Ever hear of a pusher calls himself Moses True?"

"He isn't local or I would have."

"Word is he was doing some peddling here. He took over for Johnny Ralph Dorchet about a year ago. You remember Johnny Ralph."

"I remember what was left of him on the late news. Was this True supplying the Royce girl?"

I nodded, batting away smoke. "That tooth took a little longer to pull than it should have. He's worth talking to again in the light of recent events."

"Out of my jurisdiction. Anyway, the case is morgue meat, like I said, or it is for me and Rube. The department has a rule against cops moonlighting. And I hear you're not even a P.I. these days."

"You say 'not even a P.I.' like that's lower than something stuck on a heel." I drained my can and poked my stub inside. It sighed when it touched moisture. "Would you know anything about a gold Chrysler that's been shadowing either me or Fern Esterhazy?"

"It's not us."

"What about Cecil Fish?"

"Why would he want to pin a tail on a busted peeper?"

"Why would anyone?" I got up, setting my empty down on the bench. "Thanks for talking to me. You ought to think about splitting this burg and trying your hand at police work."

"I don't think my system could stand the shock." He flashed me his thousand-candlepower smile. "The pay's sweet down in Miami, they say."

"They even throw in a free burial plot." I ducked under a B-17 Flying Fortress on my way to the door.

The air stirred by the movement started most of the suspended airplanes in the room swaying.

"What fuel you running on, Walker?"

I looked back at him. He screwed out his butt on a leg of the bench and let it drop to the floor. "You stuck your neck out for this Royce twist and got it chopped off down around the kidneys," he said.

"Fish wanted someone for the Broderick kill. Do you think Proust would have gone on looking once he had her?"

"Is that a confession? You helped her out of the country because you thought she was innocent?"

I grinned. "If it is, what good is it to you?"

"No good at all. Today. Which is why I'm not pressing it. Why are you?"

I pushed the model bomber with a finger and set it rocking. "Nice work."

After a moment he grinned.

AN OLD BLACK WOMAN WAS ARGUING WITH THE MANAGER behind the plate-glass window of the laundry on Twelfth Street, baring her dentures and shaking her fist in his crimson face. Between them, a shop model front-loader old enough to remember iron pennies drooled white foam all around the lid and down the front into a spreading puddle on the dirty linoleum. I walked past and mounted the stairs to Moses True's place. On the way through town I'd stopped at my office, and the Smith & Wesson felt as good as a hot water bottle behind my hip.

I got all the way to his door before I figured out what was wrong. Not enough dogs were barking. I knocked on the door, and still there wasn't enough barking. Nowhere near the usual amount. There was also no answer.

The animal stench seemed stronger today, even in the hall. I was breathing with my mouth open. Grasping the knob, I eased the .38 out of my waistband with the other hand. The door wasn't locked. It opened a foot and a half and stopped. A dead dog was blocking it.

It was the brown Labrador, or what was left of it after something had caved in the right side of its skull. Its curved yellow fangs were frozen in the knowing grin of death. The exposed bone, white against black blood, bore teeth marks where the surviving dogs had gnawed the jagged edge. Whoever had hit it hadn't known that its growling act was all bluff.

I stepped over the carcass. The mongrel that had attacked me lay with its back twisted, surrounded by a brackish stain on the carpet where its bowels had voided themselves. Its neck had been crushed. Threads of what looked like dark wool were pasted by blood to the pyramidal teeth in its gaping jaws. It had gone down fighting.

Corruption hung thick and sweet in the room. The yapping of the hairless mix and the deeper, kiyoodling bellow of a tragic-looking Bassett hound assumed a frantic pitch as I advanced. A slat-sided golden retriever came toward me favoring its right forepaw, sniffed my pantleg, slunk away, and lay down to lick the ragged pulp of a missing toe.

So far it was just dogs. I peeked behind the folding modesty screen that hid the toilet, checked out the kitchen area, went to a window and looked at the fire escape. Finally I grasped the bottom of the pulldown bed and tipped it up into the wall. Moses True lay fully clothed on his face on the floor where the bed had been. The starved dogs hadn't left a great deal for the medical examiner to puzzle over.

The windows were painted shut. I looked around some more until I found a wrecking bar, worked the business end under a sash, and wrenched it up far enough to let some fresh air into the room. Then I went down to the car and lost the revolver and came back up and used the telephone. We had had three deaths, some cops, dope, a mysterious tail, and two days in jail for a stubborn P.I. who was no longer a P.I., just stubborn. Now we would have some more cops.

18

I LEFT DETROIT POLICE HEADQUARTERS ON BEAUBIEN about dusk and drove back to the office. I'd had to repeat the whole story for a lieutenant named Madison, beginning with Sandy Broderick right through to my finding True's body, leaving out the favor I'd done Paula Royce and a couple of other details just to smooth out the narrative. For now the M.E. was saying death by strangulation sometime late Christmas Day or early the next morning, which thanks to Cecil Fish's hospitality left me in the clear. Nobody seemed interested in hanging me with breaking and entering a dead man's apartment, but leaving the area was something they said they'd rather I didn't do for a while. When I walked they were preparing to canvass the block for anyone who might have heard or seen something worth reporting. In that neighborhood they stood a better chance of finding one of Santa's elves left over.

It looked like another drug-related snuffing, except for the method. Drug traffickers like their guns.

My mail, which I'd ignored first time through, was

piled ankle-deep under the slot in the outer office door. I circular-filed the junk in my private tank and carried the rest—three letters—over to my desk to read. One was a late Christmas card from a former acquaintance named Iris in the West Indies, where she'd gone back to live with her mother. I read it twice and filed it with the others. It doesn't pay to have a lot of clutter lying around. The second turned out on closer inspection to be one of my own bills in its original envelope, stamped ADDRESSEE MOVED—NOT FORWARDABLE. The last bore the letterhead of the Michigan State Police in Lansing. I left it unopened while I dialed the answering service. My last official act.

"That man Horn called twice, Mr. Walker. He wouldn't leave a number."

I thanked the girl and cradled the receiver. I didn't know anyone named Horn. For a moment I sat there doing nothing. Practicing. Then I ditched the .38 and holster in the top drawer of the desk, tugged open the file drawer in the bottom, pondered the bottle of expensive Scotch—and pushed the drawer shut. I'd grown past the point where drinking helped in murder cases. The bodies were still there when the buzz wore off.

I tore open the envelope from Lansing. In response to felony charges filed by the Iroquois Heights Police Department and City Prosecutor Cecil Fish, my investigator's license and permit to carry a concealed weapon had been revoked. Failure to surrender my permit and credentials to the officer who called for them would result in my immediate arrest. The commander's signature was splashed illegibly at the bottom.

While reading through the letter a second time, I came

to the slow realization that I wasn't alone. I looked up at a thickset man in a blue suit and gray overcoat standing just inside the connecting door, which I hadn't closed. Hatless, he had very dark, very thick hair cut closely around the ears and neck but long on top, a bland, broad, unmarked face, and a huge torso slightly out of proportion with his arms and legs, which were a tad short for him. Small hands and feet. His eyes tilted down from an unremarkable nose and his complexion was very fair, so that his beard shone gunmetal blue under the skin of his cheeks and chin. For the most part his features were ordinary and about as memorable as yesterday's lunch. The only truly distinctive thing about him was a splash of white bandage showing below his shirtcuff above the hand on the doorknob, where a dog might have bitten him recently.

"You're Walker. I saw your picture in the paper." His voice was thick and soft, like a tiger's purr. "I'm Horn."

19

HE WAITED POLITELY FOR MY RESPONSE. I MADE A
thing of putting the letter from Lansing away in the top
drawer while I studied him under my lids. I didn't close
the drawer afterward. The Smith & Wesson lay inside,
its butt pointed toward me. I considered the bandage on
his wrist and remembered Moses True's dead mongrel
and the threads in its teeth.

"I'm parked at the moment, Mr. Horn," I said. "If
it's a detective you want I can recommend a couple."

His lips smiled. "No mister. Just plain Horn. I'm not
a customer. I want to talk to you about Paula Royce."

"Everyone's talking about Paula Royce this season.
I'm thinking of putting out a line of jeans with her name
on the tush. Sit down, Horn. Or can I call you Just
Plain?"

He ignored my watered-down wit, came forward, and
put a hand on the back of the customer's chair. His steps
were graceful and silent, as I'd guessed they would be.
He hesitated. "How come it's bolted down?" Suspicion
uncoiled itself under his purring tone.

"I get a lot of salesmen, most of whom have breath that would cripple a brass buffalo. I like to keep them downwind. You aren't a salesman, are you?"

He let the question die on its own. "If I prove I'm not armed, will you close that drawer?"

I said nothing. He took off his coat and folded it over a corner of the desk, the pockets on my side, unbuttoned his jacket with his left hand—the one without the bandage—opened it, turned around slowly and lifted the tails to show me he wasn't wearing a hip holster. There were sixteen other places he could be hiding a ladies' automatic, but the drawer was more convenient to me than any of those were to him. I pushed it shut. He sat down. His eyes prowled the room.

"This isn't the Oval Office," I assured him. "It's not wired."

The polite smile played around with his mouth. "Then I won't worry. Because if you say it's not and it turns out it is I'll kill you."

That's how you tell them, by the way they say kill; the way you and I say eat, sleep, and dress. The colorful euphemisms are another invention of Hollywood. I wished I hadn't closed the drawer.

"Who are you, Horn?"

"I'm someone who is looking for Paula Royce."

"Paula Royce is dead."

"Then I'm someone who is looking for Paula Royce's body. I'd rather you didn't smoke."

I'd gotten one out and was tapping it on the desk. I opened my mouth to say one of those things I'm famous for, but he cut me off.

"I'd really rather you didn't."

We watched each other. I said, "A little thing like that?"

"Little things have a way of piling up and becoming big things."

I put it back in the pack. "Who are you, Horn?"

"Excuse my rough manners." He sat back, sounding genuinely apologetic. "I just got off three years of a nickel stretch in Jackson. The guards—they call them correctional officers now—they like you to say please when you ask for something, but that's as far as it goes. I'm a working stiff, like you. I've been hired to find Paula Royce—and to make sure that anyone else who is looking for her stops."

Outside it had started to snow. I could hear the flakes sifting down onto the window sill. The temperature was too high for them to stick. So far that winter we were eighteen inches behind normal, with no change in sight. I said, "Were you also hired to find Bud Broderick?"

"They let me go Christmas Day. I was inside when his string ran out. But I read up on it. She took his Jeep and parked it around the corner from your office building. After that she fades, and she don't pop up again till they winch a stolen car out of Lake Ontario. I'd kind of like to know how she got there from here. On account of I don't think that was her."

"Have you been up there?"

He stroked the calluses on his left hand with the fingertips of his right, as if he wasn't used to having calluses there. His hands were small as I said, and as slender as a woman's. "I try to stay on this side of the border and out of small towns. That's why I came

153

straight here from Jackson after they gave me my papers. So far you haven't answered any questions.''

"So far you haven't asked any. Maybe you'd care to tell me why I should when you do.''

"I think you know why.''

"Let's stop skating and start walking, Horn. I wasn't inside long enough to cultivate your patience.''

"Remember, you asked.'' His down-tilted eyes had a sad look. And crocodiles always look like they're smiling. "Once there was a girl who said something about something that she ought not to have said anything about. My employers hired me to prevent others from making the same mistake by example. The reason they came to me and not to some others I could name is I don't get so caught up in my work I don't know when to stop. I only work when I'm getting paid. I don't like it, I don't dislike it. But because I'm good at what I do I'll do it if it's part of the job, to anyone I feel I have to if it will help me do that job. How much of this are you getting?''

"You lost me about four turns back," I said. "But I think I know where you're going. Congratulations.''

He studied my face. I hoped he wasn't getting any more out of it than I was getting from his. "What for?''

"For screwing up the language just enough so if I were taping this, the tape wouldn't be worth a dime in court. Which I'm not. Taping.''

"You screw it up pretty good yourself.'' He waited.

I knew what he was waiting for. I glanced down at my hands on the big scribble calendar that did for a blotter. My fingertips were white around purple nails. I unclamped them, leaving little indentations throughout the middle week of December. "I'll give you what I gave the cops. It's public record anyway. I don't know where Paula Royce is. I didn't know where she was when I was in jail, and all I know about where she is now you can get from tonight's paper. Officially her book is closed, which means I have no reason to hold back. As of just a few minutes ago I don't even have a license to stand in front of."

"You haven't been listening." He leaned forward in his seat, placing his hands on the desk. They were nowhere near as large as mine, and as clean and pink and hairless as a mannequin's. They fascinated me. The bandage was a sudden white gash at the base of his right palm. "Being locked up can be like dying. In some ways it's worse, especially at night. But you come back from there, that's the difference. You come back from there."

His voice didn't change, and his complexion remained fair just this side of pale. But I'd come within touching distance of armed Vietcong and I'd never stood that close to the rim. I held his eyes with mine while I used my knee to work open the desk drawer from the bottom.

Keep his attention. "That looks nasty," I said, nodding at the dressing on his wrist. "Dog bite you?"

"I caught it on a nail. Go ahead, stall. I've got patience, like you said. As long as I leave with what I came for."

The drawer caught on one of the runners with a flatulent noise. I spoke loudly to cover it.

"I saw the nail you caught yourself on. What sort of hammer did you use on it?"

155

Something dark and empty with no bottom opened behind his pupils. I had some of the drawer out, I couldn't tell how much. It had to be enough. I wouldn't try to clear the gun; I'd fire it right through the desk and take a chance on the bullet's glancing off something. The noise might be enough. I moved.

He moved faster. His hands were flat on the desk top, and then they were gripping my wrists. That fast. He didn't even have all his fingers around them, they weren't long enough to encircle them. Only his thumbs and forefingers were pressing the hollows in front of the bony knobs at the breaks. But I couldn't move. Numbness crawled toward my fingers. Moses True's mongrel and Sergeant Zorn's handcuffs hadn't held me any tighter. I looked at the empty dark yawning maw behind his pupils and I couldn't move.

"There are a hundred and six ways to kill a man without weapons," he said. "A hundred and six. I haven't tried them all yet."

The blood couldn't get to my hands. I could feel its angry frustrated surging, could hear the *thrum-thrum-thrum* of my pulse amplified by the pressure holding it back, like the noise of a destroyer's screws passing within depth-charge range of a submarine in an old war movie. It wasn't hypnosis. It was the awesome proximity of nonexistence.

"What do you want?"

I wondered who had said that. It wasn't a voice I recognized. Later I'd tell myself I was just buying time to think, but I wasn't. I'd have tossed him my mother to pull myself back from that gaping hole.

"Where is she?" Same conversational tone as before.

If there was any effort at all behind his grasp he was good at hiding it.

"I don't know."

He held on for a beat. I didn't care. I couldn't feel anything below my wrists anyway. Then he sat back, drawing his hands back and laying them on his knees. But the phantom pressure of his thumbs and forefingers remained.

"I believe you." He rose. From where I sat he was as tall as a factory stack. Actually he was probably my height. He lifted his coat off the desk and shoved his fists into the sleeves. It wasn't tailored like his suit, and the cuffs hung to his fingers. He looked down at me speculatively. "You never met anyone like me before, did you?"

So he had vanity. It made me fear him a little less, but not enough less to try again for the revolver in the desk. I resisted the urge to rub circulation back into my hands and met his gaze. "Mechanics come a penny a carload in this town," I snarled. "I've met the hard eggs with their coat collars turned up and their hands in their pockets and ventriloquist's lips that only let them talk out of the sides of their mouths. I've dealt with the cowboys who can't talk without a lot of knuckle-cracking and two packs of spearmint snapping between their molars, and I've bandied words with the funny-funny boys who kick the comic-book slang around like a sissy quoting Shakespeare and whose brains you couldn't find with a magnifying glass, and after you found them you couldn't pick them up with tweezers. The preppie types with guns in their briefcases and the same upwardly mobile junior executive look just bore me. I've had them all, the nuts who like to see them squirm just before they bust the cap and the tired pros with families waiting for them at home who think Daddy's on a sales trip to Houston. Occasionally, not as seldom as I'd like, I run into the jeeters with skinfuls of hop and so much firepower in their fists they can't hold them still. They scare me the most, because they can't predict what they're going to do next any better than I can. Next to them you mild ones who won't threaten a person except in the most general terms are so much spent wind. Maybe I never met anyone like you, or maybe I did and I just don't remember because they didn't make that much of an impression.''

"That's quite a pep talk you give yourself." He buttoned his coat with his good hand. I was glad I'd caught him when they weren't both good. "You're scared, all right. You just carry it better than most. I've read enough psychology to pick up a degree if I wanted to attract that many flies. Being afraid's nothing to be ashamed of. The rest of you draw lines for yourselves you won't cross. When you meet someone who doesn't observe any, fear is a natural reaction."

I yawned.

He said "Ha" involuntarily, and moved to the door without turning around. When he got there I said, "You don't happen to own a gold LeBaron, do you?"

"I don't own a gold anything. My driver's license expired my second year in the can. Why?"

I shrugged.

He squinted at me a moment longer, then let go. "I'm going to go on looking for Paula Royce," he said. "The other half of my job is to see no one else does."

His chest swelled, and then he spun on his left foot and lashed out horizontally with his right, snapping the leg perpendicular to his body. The ball of his foot struck the edge of the connecting door, splintering the heavy crossbar and shattering the pebbled glass. Furnaces explode with less noise.

"That's one. There are a hundred and five more where that came from." He backed out, footsteps crunching on the broken glass. He moved like someone who was used to leaving rooms that way.

I waited until the door to the outer office closed against the pressure of the pneumatic closer, then got out the gun and the bottle and put them both on top of the desk. My hands had been steadier.

20

I FORCED MYSELF TO DRINK SLOWLY. ALCOHOL BLESSED alcohol. Makes lions out of mice, and when applied properly allows a frightened ex-snooper to use the telephone, provided he speaks more slowly than he drinks and holds the receiver in both fists. The office was growing dark. I switched on the desk lamp, which just made the shadows more ominous. I started to dial Barry Stackpole's private number at the *News*, forgot it, looked it up in the special book I kept locked in the file cabinet, and tried again. No one knew local talent better than Barry, whose column on organized crime was syndicated throughout the country.

"Stackpole."

"Like hell," I said after a pause. "I know Barry's voice since Nam and this ain't it."

"This is Gable Reinhardt, his research assistant." The voice was a good ten years younger than Barry's, almost boyish. I pictured Jimmy Olsen, bow tie and freckles.

"Why didn't you say so in the first place?"

"Would you, if your name was Gable Reinhardt?"

"Where's Barry, who never to my knowledge had a research assistant until this moment?"

"He asked for a raise. He got me. He's under cover right now, working on a story. Who is this?"

I told him who it was.

"No shit?" He spoke more quickly. "I read where you were in jail."

"They let me out when they clean my cage. Where can I reach Barry?"

"You can't. Under cover is under cover. I can't even get a message to him. What's the story?"

"Who am I talking to, you or your sheet?"

"Me, when you put it that way, damn it."

I sighed. Well, I was a free agent now. "What do you know about heavyweights in these parts?"

"Not much. Try Sports."

"I'm not talking about fighters. I mean mechanics. Lifetakers. Soldiers. Button men. Choose your own cute name for people who kill other people for pay."

"Okay, I know what you mean. I just wanted to hear you say it. Pros or part-timers?"

"Pros."

"I've got some stuff. I don't know that it's current."

"This one's been out of circulation a while."

"What you paying?"

I lit a weed. "You Lou Grant types do like your meat lean. I'll try to swing something your way when this breaks."

"And I'd have to run it under Stackpole's byline. Forget it. He doesn't need my help. How about fifty?"

"Dollars?"

"No, pencils." His tone would etch steel. "I've got

a week to cough up child support or I start the new year with numbers on my shirt.''

''Twenty. If the information's good.''

''I wouldn't get out of this chair for twenty, and it's got a busted spring. Fifty, no guarantees. This isn't negotiable. I don't look good in gray.''

''Prisoners aren't wearing gray this year, take it from me.'' I leaked smoke. ''Fifty it is. But I'll tell Barry.''

''He'll be sore I didn't cut him in. But, hell, I'm going into TV anyway. What about this snuffer?''

''I can't describe him. I just met him and already I forgot what he looks like. He said his name was Horn.''

Silence crackled. Under the dead air on his end I heard the clatter of a distant typewriter. Probably a secretary in the legal department writing a letter. It used to be all typewriters down there, but the whole world's gone drunk on computers.

I said, ''Reinhardt?''

''Sorry. Not Fletcher Horn?''

''We didn't get to first names.''

Another pause, shorter. ''Let's meet.''

''Suits me. Barry's office?''

''Not with these walls. You know the Sextant Bar on West Lafayette? It's between the *News* and the *Free Press*.''

''Well enough to count my change after I've paid for a drink.''

''Seven o'clock?''

I checked my watch. ''Make it seven-thirty. I haven't eaten since stir.''

''Bring cash.''

I hung up carefully. I was starting to feel the Scotch,

which is what two days' enforced abstention will do for you. For a moment I considered pouring what was in my glass back into the bottle, then decided I couldn't do that without spilling any and dumped it into a larger container instead. I felt it strike bottom. If my feet touched the broken glass on my way out of the office I didn't feel it. I locked the outer door.

THE SEXTANT WAS A NARROW WALK-IN JAMMED BE-tween office buildings equidistant from the last two big-city dailies in the United States who were still trying to cut each other's throat, with a canvas canopy erected out front in honor of Queen Victoria's Diamond Jubilee and a row of booths inside separated by a footworn aisle from the stools at the bar. A barmaid wearing a platinum cap of hair and too much make-up was smoking a little cigar in the first booth, across from a middle-aged man whose ink-smeared coveralls identified him as a press operator for one of the papers. The only other customer was a skinny kid with a receding hairline and wire-rimmed glasses nursing a drink in the back booth. I went over there and slid into the seat opposite.

"You look like a Gable Reinhardt," I said.

He eyed me from under heavy lids behind his glasses. He was wearing sparse muttonchop whiskers and a threadbare combat jacket. He didn't look old enough to have served in the army, but then he didn't look old enough to have been married and divorced either, and fathered a child in the bargain. "How was supper?"

"Burned and late. It's nice to be free." I ordered Scotch and water from the barmaid, who had ditched the stogie and her companion. Reinhardt stood pat.

When she had gone, he said: "There's no resemblance."

"To what?"

"Not what, who. Galahad. Sir Walter. Don Quixote; take your pick. You don't look like any of them, and nobody else would go into the tank for a chick."

"That what they're saying around the *News*?"

"They're not near as polite. Why did you, really?"

"Off the record?"

He shrugged. "I don't work where I drink."

"Proust and Fish could have had what they wanted if they'd bothered to treat me like a citizen instead of an accomplice. But they didn't, so they didn't."

He was still waiting for more when the barmaid brought our drinks. I laid some money on the table and watched her walk away with it, then: "Horn."

"Fifty bucks."

I showed him a bill. Before he could get his hands on it, I smoothed it out on the table and stood my glass atop U.S. Grant's stern countenance. Sat back, set some tobacco on fire, waited. Every move pure poetry. I was so sick of the whole dumb-show I could kiss Proust for delivering me from it.

"My information says he's in Jackson," said the research assistant.

"He's out."

He nodded, just to be doing something. "His name probably isn't Horn. He's Canadian, or was. State Department tried deporting him a few years back over some lies he told on his application for citizenship, but they weren't such big lies and no one's been able to pin him to a homicide yet."

"How many homicides haven't they been able to pin him to?"

"Eight anyway. That's just since the cops started counting. One even got to a grand jury."

"Let me guess," I said. "Witness lost his memory."

"What witness?"

I searched his narrow features. "He's that good?"

"He's two police guards in a downtown hotel good. They went to roust their witness out of the bathroom for his day in court and found him ducking for apples in the toilet bowl. Drowned."

"Not very original."

"There aren't any original ways left. From the variety of the killings, your man is proficient in firearms, demolitions, and cutting edges, but he appears to prefer his bare hands. He's as strong as a bull and he has the equivalent of a black belt in karate."

"No kidding. How'd he end up on ice?"

"Dime store stuff." The reporter touched his lips to his glass for the first time since I'd sat down. "They lifted his thumbprint off the wheel of a Pontiac he boosted when the car he was using to crash a hit at Metro Airport laid down on him. It wasn't solid enough to tack him to the kill, but the D.A. thought he might save a life or two by sticking him in the shade for a little."

"It doesn't hang straight," I said. "A guy that can nudge a guy under police guard doesn't leave a good print on a stolen crate."

"Not unless he wanted a vacation. The stiff in the hotel wasn't virgin. He had friends. Even the Al Kaline of hit men can wear lead from a punk with a Saturday

Night Buster and the price of a lid in his pocket. It's been done."

"I just talked to you an hour ago. How'd you scrape all this together so fast?"

He sat back and sipped his something-and-tonic. I lifted my glass and pushed the fifty across the table. It went into one of the flap pockets of his jacket.

"The file was pulled already," he said. "Barry wanted all he could get on freelancers that have worked this area before he went underground."

I paused with the glass halfway to my lips. "What's he working?"

"I don't know that fifty goes that far."

I set down the glass and reached over and took hold of his collar in one hand and twisted it. "I'm a P.I. with a busted license who just capped two days behind bars in my favorite county this side of Devil's Island with a threat to have my lights put out by someone who knows a hundred and six ways to do it without a weapon. I don't much care how far fifty goes, or how many times I have to hit this table with your head until you figure it out. Are you getting all this?"

The room was very quiet, but not like the second floor of the brick building in downtown Iroquois Heights was quiet. I could feel the barmaid and the press operator and the thin party behind the bar watching us. Gable Reinhardt's glass lay on its side on the table, its contents running down into his lap. He didn't appear to be paying it any attention. His face matched the maroon vinyl upholstery of the high seat behind his head. He managed to nod quickly. I let go of his collar.

"Drugs," he gasped.

"Drugs what?"

He shook his head, still gasping. I righted his glass and signaled the barmaid. She hesitated, then brought over a full one and took away the empty without looking at either of us. The usual bar noise resumed. I watched the research assistant put down half his drink without stopping. Then he used his napkin to mop off his lap. I finished my cigarette and fired up another while he was doing all this.

"Barry's convinced a new organization is moving in on the drug trade in Detroit," he said, looking at my left ear. "It started when Johnny Ralph Dorchet and his partners got gunned last December. Ten days later the cops scraped a family of pushers off the walls of a house in Redford Township, and then a trafficker the feds were getting set to bust on a tax beef got himself clubbed and gassed to death in his garage on Watson. Since then a couple of wild cards have turned up that may or may not tie in. Cops bought a conviction in one of them, but Barry thinks he was a stalking horse. He's out digging for some hard answers."

"What makes it new talent?" I asked. "These gang things blow up every couple of years."

"It's the pattern. Every time a new family moves into the neighborhood they bring in the Prohibition stuff, make a lot of noise. Then when they get a foothold they quiet down. They yank the cowboys, rely more on mechanics like your boy Horn to mop up. Not so many headlines. Each group thinks they invented it, but it happened the same way in New York and Chicago in the twenties when the Italians took over, and again when the blacks cruised in here ten years ago. It's happening now with the Cubans and Colombians down in Miami.''

He was warming to his subject. He'd forgotten all about my mussing him up. Kid journalists are the ones to latch on to. They're always busting to tell someone the story they can't print yet.

I emptied my glass thoughtfully. "Where does Moses True hang his hat in all this? He got dusted the other day, probably by Horn.''

"I hadn't heard.'' He was wiping his glasses with a fresh napkin. His hooded eyes were a little fuzzy. He didn't seem surprised by the news. "Barry predicted something like that. True was a stopgap to smooth the transition between the old and the new. He was more flexible than Dorchet. He wouldn't care whose money he was spending. But he would be temporary, and this bunch pays everyone off in the same coin.''

"Who is the new kid on the block?'' I twirled a finger inside the rim of my empty glass and made it wobble, keeping my eyes down so he couldn't see the gleam in them. That could be expensive.

"We'll know that when Barry comes up for air.'' His tone dripped smug. "But have you noticed all the fresh Spanish accents around this town lately?''

"Colombians?''

He smiled.

A loose spring snapped into place in the back of my head. I felt flushed, but not from the Scotch. I got up quickly. Reinhardt started slightly at the sudden movement.

"Thanks.'' I paid for his drink. "Sorry about the rough trade.''

"That's okay. For another fifty you can break my arm if you want."

"Another time, maybe."

I met the barmaid in the aisle. She smiled, cracking the powder on her cheeks. "I'd of paid money to see that," she said in a low voice. "That little punk is always jacking somebody up in here for somebody else's dirt."

"Glad to be of service."

"I'm usually pretty good on faces. I don't remember yours."

"It's just a face."

She said, "I get off at ten."

"I don't blame you. It's a good number."

She was still puzzling it out when I left her.

My car was in a lighted city lot a block down from the *News* building. On my way to the booth I stopped to admire a gold Chrysler LeBaron cranked into a slot two cars down. The attendant was busy, so I opened the passenger's door and leafed through the usual junk in the glove compartment until I found the registration. It was made out to Theodore Grundy. Of course I didn't know anyone by that name.

21

THE ATTENDANT WAS A SHORT ROUND BLACK WEARING a faded red parka over a denim jacket over a sweatshirt over a flannel shirt over a thermal top with a hole chewed in the neckband. He catalogued me from behind thick horn-rimmed glasses as I approached his booth.

"Silver Olds, right?" he said.

"Right. Say, that's quite a memory you have."

He beamed, the tip of a pale pink tongue showing through the gap where his front teeth belonged, and took my keys off a peg under the window. "Sixty-five cents."

I gave him a buck, collected my keys, and watched him make change from the dingus on his belt. "Bet you can't describe the guy that belongs to that Chrysler." I pointed my chin at it.

His lids came down, but he was watching me through the lashes. He played with the coins, clicking them together. "Depends on the bet."

"Another buck on top of the change."

He said, "That's him pretending to tie his shoelace." I turned away to cough. A slim number with a dark moustache in a gray three-piece and leather trenchcoat had one foot propped up on the bumper of a green Toronado and was fiddling with his shoe. He was wearing loafers.

I gave the attendant another bill. "How much to lose his keys for five minutes?"

"A buck a minute. It's the job if he complains to the city."

"The hell it is. The city hasn't canned anyone since Cavanaugh was mayor." But I tipped him five.

He pocketed it along with the other bill and my change, lifted a ring of keys off a peg, dropped it into his change drawer, and bumped the drawer shut with his hard round stomach. I pointed an index finger at him with thumb cocked and made a snicking noise out the side of my mouth. He gave me back his cat's-grin with his tongue showing. I turned around and walked past Slim to my machine. He finished adjusting his pantcuff and strolled over to the booth, whistling loudly. He had to be a fed. No one else carries airy nonchalance like it's a sack of anvils.

He was arguing with the attendant when I backed out of my space and rolled out past him onto Lafayette. I turned east, hung a right onto Washington on the yellow, made another right onto Congress, and parked in a loading zone near the lot's back entrance. Before climbing out I flipped down the visor with my honorary sheriff's star pinned to it. It might confuse a cop long enough for me to get back before he called the wrecker.

My shadow was still too busy shouting obscenities at the guy in the booth to notice me hurrying along the other aisle. I let myself into his car and got down on the floor between the front and back seats and waited with my Smith & Wesson in my hand.

After a couple of minutes I heard rapid footsteps scraping asphalt and the door on the driver's side was torn open and a body flung heavily into the seat. Keys jingled. I sat up and touched the gun's cold muzzle to the back of a slender neck.

"Slow down, Ted," I said quietly. "Or is it Theo?"

He took it well, just a little reddening at the base of his scalp and around the edges of his ears. I nudged him gently with the barrel to stop him before he got started. He relaxed just enough.

"It's Theodore." His voice was deep and full, as slim men's often are. "I hate nicknames."

"Hands on the wheel, Theodore."

He complied, placing them precisely at ten and two. Somehow I was sure he would. I switched hands on the gun quickly and slid my right under his arm and around his chest. He had a .22 target pistol under his left armpit. That meant he was good, or wanted others to think he was. I laid it on the seat beside me and got his ID folder out of an inside pocket. The card said he was with the Justice Department. I flipped the folder onto the front seat and sat back, still covering him but holding the gun down where it couldn't be seen easily from outside.

"Why the tail?" I asked. "I pay taxes, when I make enough to have taxes to pay."

He started to take his hands off the wheel. I advised him to leave them there. He said, "Can we go somewhere? This is like a fish tank."

"Uh-uh. Mama didn't raise me to threaten other people with deadly weapons and then put them in charge of deadlier ones. This is Detroit. No one would look twice if I painted the windshield with your brains and then yanked your wheel covers and tape deck. I said why the tail and why the tail is what I said.''

"I'm just an employee. I was told to follow you and report on your movements and contacts. I wasn't told why.''

"Oh lie. Go again.''

"I'm telling the tru—''

I grabbed a fistful of hair at the nape of his neck and bounced his head off the steering wheel. It sounded like someone kicking a tire.

"You dumb shit, I'm a feder—''

I bounced him again.

"You know what the pen—''

Again. This time the horn peeped. "We can do this all day," I said. I was still holding him by the hair. "I'm unemployed, I've got the time. How about we go halves? I'll tell you what I think's going down as far as I've got it figured. You tell me how wrong I am. Sort of like comparing notes. You do that sometimes." I let go.

"When you put it that way—''

"Yeah." I sat back again. "Ready?''

He was busy rearranging his black hair over a small bald spot in back. His eyes met mine in the rearview mirror. He nodded.

"Your interest is Paula Royce," I began.

He said nothing. So far I was on target.

"She told me once she was from Bolivia, but she wasn't. She was Colombian. I'll get back to that later.

She's being tracked by a killer named Horn who doesn't
think she's dead, but who wants to make sure because
she once talked too much about something and she has
to be made an example of so that no one else gets the
same idea. The reason I think she's Colombian is it's
the Colombians who are muscling in on the drug racket
in Detroit. They're the only Spanish-speaking people
with the background and connections to undertake the
job. They bumped a local dealer named Dorchet along
with two of his associates because he wouldn't listen to
reason, put Moses True in his place because he would
and because of his recognition factor among the customers, then had him bumped too when he outlived his
usefulness. Horn again. He's the peg I'm hanging all
this on. You knew about True?''

He kept silent.

"I'm on shakier ground here, so let me know when
I step wrong. Paula Royce's history goes back eighteen
months and stops. Even the Iroquois Heights cops can't
go any deeper, and this is the age of computers. Her
prints go to Washington and nothing comes back. No
one person is that good at hiding his past. Only the
government can do that, and it's a specialty of the Justice Department. Paula Royce, who is not named Royce
at all, testified against some of her compatriots in the
drug trade, probably though not necessarily in Miami,
in return for a new identity and relocation courtesy of
Uncle Sam, with a steady allowance thrown in so that
she doesn't have to work for a living. She told me herself she had an outside source of income. Her nation-
ality was changed for extra protection and she was given
that dumb story about her parents having been killed in

an automobile accident, just in case someone asked about her family. That was unworthy of you fellows; a real paste-up job.''

''No, that part's true,'' Theodore Grundy broke in. ''Her parents actually were killed that way. We like to incorporate bits and pieces of a witness's actual past where we can, for authenticity.''

''Could be you were right. It's just corny enough to be swallowed by anyone but a suspicious private star. Where you fell down was in failing to cure her of her dependence on prescription drugs. Dorchet was supplying her, or at least he was supplying the parties she went to in Grosse Pointe, until the takeover, when True replaced him. Somewhere along the line True got on to his new employers' interest in Paula, because he took the trouble to find out where she lived. My thought is he sold them the information and then they sicked one of their cowboys on her.

''He botched the job, as cowboys will. I read it that Paula's roommate, Bud Broderick, got iced trying to protect her and that the killer panicked and ran without doing the job he came to do. Now the Colombians had to forget about her until things simmered down, and clean up. True knew what had gone down and he was a semi-outsider. This trip they waited until real talent was available, and then they didn't waste any time. Horn got out of stir Christmas Day. Next morning True was literally dog meat. Which leaves just one question.

''Where's Paula Royce?''

''She's dead.''

''That's my line,'' I said. ''I used it on Horn for the same reason, and he didn't believe it any more than I did. Somebody in your department has his record stuck, Grundy. Too many people in her family died in traffic accidents. If she did, you wouldn't be shadowing me. And that brings me back to what I started with. Why the tail?''

He averted his eyes from the mirror, drummed fingers on the edge of the wheel, looked back at my reflection. ''The alias program is one of the strongest weapons we have, Walker. Your poking around threatens to uncover too many of the seams. If how it works gets to be public knowledge we're back where we were at the time of the old Kefauver Committee hearings. You wouldn't remember those.''

''I would, barely. You wouldn't. According to your ID you were born the year they would have aired on television. Feed me the rest.''

''The point is they weren't very effective, short of kicking off a short-lived campaign to nominate Senator Kefauver for President. The witnesses that could have made a difference there and in similar investigations later were afraid to step forward. It wasn't until we had developed a system whereby we could offer a ninety-nine percent guarantee of protection from reprisal that we began winning indictments against leading figures in organized crime. The program is—''

''I know what it is. This isn't a high school auditorium. What you're trying hard not to say is that your precious program's fate rests on the fates of the witnesses you help take a powder. You can't afford the headlines if somebody gets to one of them. For some reason, maybe because it was Christmas Eve, Paula Royce wasn't able to get hold of a fed the night Broderick was killed in her own house and she knew her cover was blown. So she came to me and asked me to get her the hell away from the area fast. She let me know what had happened, but she didn't confide the rest, because she had every reason to believe that Yankee Doodle Dandy would be able to take over in a day or so when all the wrapping paper was in the incinerator and the leftover turkey was eaten. And she was right. Two days after I drove her into Windsor so she could crash in a nonexistent cabin belonging to Bud's stepfather—Mrs. Esterhazy would have told me about it when Bud was missing if there were such a place—while I was cooling my heels in the tank, 'Paula Royce' went into Lake Ontario and Thelma Ingolstadt, or whatever new name you gave her, was whisked away to Wyoming or some such place equally inaccessible. You haven't told me I'm wrong so far.''

''You haven't given me much chance.'' He drummed his fingers again. ''If what you say is true—and I'm not saying for one minute that it is—her safety would depend on your going home and forgetting about her. That would be one good reason why I'm following you, to make sure you do. It doesn't appear that you have.''

''There's a little matter of my license,'' I said. ''My license which I don't got no more on account of I was there to help out when you weren't.''

''I've been wondering about that. She helped us because the bunch we were after killed her brother, who was a low-level guard on their drug shipments until they found out he was funneling some of it off for his own business on the side. We helped her because her testimony was instrumental in breaking up one of the biggest drug rings in Florida. Why did you agree to help her? What did you have to gain?"

"It was Christmas."

His eyes in the mirror looked confused.

"Forget it. Let's just say it's not all Gene Autry and hysterical reminders in the newspaper about how many shopping days are left." I holstered my .38. "I take it you know as much about who pulled the trigger on Bud Broderick as I do."

"We don't have any interest in finding out. He was never our concern."

"Even if the killer is your star witness?"

He was looking at me over the back of the seat now. His moustache twisted. "They call us the Justice Department. It's just a name. No one expects us to live up to it."

I gave him that one. I'd have had to untangle it before I could top it anyway. I broke the clip out of his automatic, ejected the shell from the chamber, stuck it in the clip, and dropped the gun on the front seat. "So long, Grundy. I've told me all I need to know." I tossed the clip onto the ledge under the back window and opened the door.

"Just a second," he said. "Are you going to continue looking for Paula Royce?"

"As long as Horn is. It has something to do with my picking up a key early on a holiday morning. It doesn't matter that it was a phony. You wouldn't understand."

I got out and slammed the door. He cranked down the window on his side. The glass had frosted over just since we'd been talking. He blinked up at me in the glare of a spot mounted on a pole overhead. "I'm not making any promises. I have to speak with my superiors. Suppose things could be fixed so you got your license back. Would that interest you at all?''

"I hear you talking, Mr. Grundy."

He smiled the crooked smile. "I thought you might. You'll be hearing from us."

He rolled the window back up and started the engine. I stood watching as he backed around and left, one rear tire spinning a little on a slick spot on the pavement. I trotted back to my car. The badge on the visor had bought me a ticket for parking in a loading zone, nothing else.

22

CALL IT CLAIRVOYANCE OR CRACKPOT RECKONING OR A
dream's passing shadow, but it happens. At ten past
three the next morning I sat straight up in bed, convinced that Paula Royce was still in the area.

I told myself those things you trot out when a batty
idea keeps you awake. I was wrong to begin with, and
even if I was right there was nothing I could do about
it right away, and probably not at all, and even if I could
what business was it of mine? That didn't work. It had
never been any business of mine from the start.

Why was the Justice Department burning good daylight tailing a busted cop? Not, as Theodore Grundy had
intimated, because they were afraid I'd foul their pon-
derous machinery single-handed. Even Congress
couldn't do that, although it had tried often enough. If
I were that much of a danger, they could have taken me
out of the picture in less time than it takes a waiter to
spit in your eye after you've tipped him a quarter. A
search of my car alone would turn up the unregistered

Luger, which in Michigan is good for a year of planting trees along state highways if the judge feels like leaning.

The papers had filled plenty of space from the official police line that I was the last person to see Paula after Bud Broderick was murdered. The Justice Department, which had a vested interest in her well-being, had then hung a shadow on me. Why? In the hope I'd lead them to where she was hiding. They'd moved fast to rig her death, but that was just a temporary measure to buy time while they located her and spirited her away from harm. Now that they knew I wasn't cooperating they were going to dangle my license under my nose, and if the carrot failed the stick was next. I'd told Grundy I didn't know where she was, but guys in his line lie so much about their identities and occupations you couldn't expect them to recognize the truth if it came up and wet their pantlegs.

The girl had gotten a good dose of just how badly the system could fail when it failed. This time through she decided to trust no one but herself and a P.I. who had nothing to gain from betraying her, and she hadn't trusted him enough to hand him the whole story. She'd skipped the country until things hotted down, but she'd be back, if only long enough to make connections for parts unknown. It wasn't as easy to be a fugitive in Canada as it had been at the height of the war in Vietnam. She'd know that. She was smarter than all of us. Smart enough to outsmart herself and land square in the jaws of a hunting thing like Horn.

Around five o'clock I gave up on sleep, climbed into my robe and slippers, and sat down in front of the set to watch a late-late showing of a movie starring George

Sanders as The Falcon. I dropped off before he solved the murder and woke up at seven in time for a kiddie show. Next I'd be following the soaps along with all the other hardcore unemployables. I switched off the set and grumped into the bathroom for repairs.

The telephone rang while I was reading about Moses True's murder in the *Free Press* after breakfast. Sergeant Somebody of the Michigan State Police post at Northville wanted to know if I'd be in my office later that morning before he sent around a trooper to confiscate my license, CCW permit, and wallet credentials. I said yeah and hung up in his face. But I was glad he'd called. I'd begun to feel like the widow whose life was in suspension until she could get her husband's remains into the ground and out of the way.

IN THE LIGHT OF DAY, MY THEORY CONCERNING PAULA Royce was as full of holes as a catcher's mask. Even if she had come back, and even if she couldn't book a flight out during the holidays, she'd have cleared the area fast if she had to do it on foot. It wasn't until I got to the office and saw again the wreckage of my door that I gave the hunch any weight at all. Horn thought as I did or he wouldn't have hung around Detroit just to scare the hell out of me. He would at least have gone to Canada to see if he could get a line on her from there. He was a native, after all. His story about avoiding small towns and border crossings was just a story.

I called down to maintenance for a new door. I told Rosecranz, the superintendent, that a professional killer had trashed it by way of showing off. Rosecranz told me to lay off the sauce and I wouldn't walk into so many doors, and said he'd bill me after the job was done. I don't know why I bothered. Maybe I could hang astrology charts on the walls and take up telling fortunes. It was bound to pay better than what I'd been doing.

The mail came just before ten. Season's greetings from two city council members up for re-election, a bill, a magazine sweepstakes, a once-in-a-lifetime offer for an eight-week correspondence course in fingerprinting, and a calendar from my bonding company. I kept the bill and the calendar and tipped everything else into the wastebasket.

My mind was growing weeds. I broke out a deck of cards for some heavy thinking. Sherlock Holmes's fiddle had nothing on clock solitaire. I was placing a red trey on a black four when I remembered Arthur Stillson.

When I was still recovering from the headache she'd handed me at her place, I'd babbled something to Paula about the lawyer's side racket involving phony IDs. She was a person who would remember a reference like that when the need arose, and from her experience with the Justice Department she would know just what was required. With a complete new set of papers and a new hairdo she could walk through a double row of hawk-eyed cops and board a plane for anywhere.

I looked up Stillson's number in the Iroquois Heights book and got a female voice as smooth and hard as polished steel that informed me he was vacationing in the Bahamas and wouldn't be back until after the first of the year. I thanked her and the conversation was over. I wasn't disappointed. If I had to wait so did Paula. And if she had to wait, sooner or later she would have to get in touch with Rhett Grissom.

Grissom was the rich kid I'd mussed up about a hundred years ago in Grosse Pointe to find out who was supplying Paula with pills. She would still need them, and with Moses True treading clouds Grissom was the next likely source. If anyone had seen her since Windsor it would be him. I left the cards where they were and snatched my coat and hat off the peg on my way out. On the stairs I passed Rosecranz heading up to my floor with a steel tape measure.

A HIGH SMALL SUN SHONE ALMOST STRAIGHT DOWN onto the lake, its rays flashing off the choppy cobalt surface. The buildings on the foreign side, glowering on my last visit, looked as scrubbed and bright as children's faces on Easter morning. Across from them, Detroit was a reflection in a dirty mirror. The garage next to the Grissoms' Victorian manse was closed and there was no sign of the snowmobile I'd trashed. Rhett probably had two more on order. As I got out of the car, a miserable-looking seagull with wings streaked brown turned a round black eye on me from its roost on a gullproof roof pike, leaned forward, and twisted its tail to show me what it thought of such precautions.

"Good for you," I said, stepping up onto the round wooden porch.

The door looked like a giant Hershey bar, deep brown and paneled. It had a screw-you window the size of a jeweler's eyepiece that was as much Renaissance Detroit as it was nineteenth-century London. I pressed a mother-of-pearl button and waited for an eye to appear. When none did I pressed again, then knocked, and I was still waiting. I tried the knob. It gave. I had a premonition. I was going to make a discovery I would regret.

The front parlor—"living room" didn't quite do it—was large enough to make a lot of antique furniture look like a little, skylit, and paved to within six inches of the walls with a bland rug that was as old as Christianity and just had to have cost as much as some houses. It reminded me of home, if home were an exhibit at the Detroit Historical Museum. The other rooms on the ground floor were almost as big, every bit as stiff and expensively furnished, and just as empty of Rhett Grissom. The kitchen looked as it had the last time I was in it. There was a room on the second floor that had been a ballroom but now contained spoiled plants flourishing in fat pots, two bedrooms half as large, and a den in a tower room overlooking the lake. A matronly lady with thick arms and legs in a maid's uniform and fluffy gray hair under a white cap was bent over a glass-topped desk in the den, shoving around a chamois dust cloth for all she was worth. She straightened, turned, saw me, and jumped twelve feet. She had a thick East European nose and blue eyes that were faded and frightened.

"Rhett's friend?" she inquired hopefully. Living in Hamtramck as long as I had been, I knew a Polish accent when I heard it.

"Kind of," I said, when I remembered what my tongue was for. Old Hawkshaw here hadn't expected to run into a maid in a Grosse Pointe mansion. "I rang and knocked. No one answered."

"What?"

I said it all again. She repeated, "What?" That time I got the message. "Where's Rhett?" I shouted it.

"People walk in, people walk out, all the time. In, out like a hotel. Parties. Parties day and night. A burglar could walk in, a sex fiend, how'd I know he isn't Rhett's friend?"

"Rhett," I bellowed. "Where is he?"

"Rhett's friend?"

I was living an ethnic joke. "Where is Rhett?" Long pauses between words as I wrote them in the air.

"Where's Rhett?"

I nodded. My hat shook loose. I caught it and jammed it back on.

"Where's Rhett, how'd I know where's Rhett? Two, t'ree days no Rhett, then party. Who cleans up after Rhett's parties? Not Rhett."

"Okay if I look around for him?"

"What?"

I waved good-bye.

The place had four bathrooms. He wasn't in any of them. I went outside through the kitchen. The garage and the boat house were locked, the latter with a padlock on the outside. Through the garage window I saw a yellow Lamborghini and a black-and-silver Eldorado and some odds and ends of garage stuff, spotless rags and tools that didn't look as if they'd ever been used. The Eldorado would be for winter driving so the Italian job wouldn't rust out. The crunched snowmobile was parked between them. He hadn't repaired it yet. The bath house down by the lake was open and empty. I wandered around the grounds and out to the end of the wharf. The view was pretty even in winter. The water made little slurping sounds on the sandy shore.

I almost walked back up the dock to leave. I can't

say why I didn't. Call it instinct or gut feeling or just that same atavistic caution that makes a child look under his bed before going to sleep. I got down on my knees on aging boards slimy with fish scales and guano and curled my fingers around the edge and peered underneath. At first I didn't see anything. Then my eyes grew accustomed to the dim light reflecting up off the water and casting crawling haloes on the dark underside of the dock and the thing trapped there and bobbing on the polite tide.

Our faces were close enough to kiss, but I didn't indulge. The thing's blond hair was dark and plastered to some swollen meat that may or may not have been the face of one Rhett Grissom. Splintered bone poked through the torn flesh in places. I'd seen one like that in Vietnam, when my squad entered a hut that had been used by Charlie to interrogate captured prisoners before bugging out. Over there it had been part of the natural order of things. In my own backyard it was different.

And one thing was sure. He hadn't drowned, not floating on his back like that. But if he had he would have welcomed it.

I stood up and brushed the dirt off my knees and cast my eyes around the lake that was actually only a lull in the Detroit River. The buildings of Windsor still looked clean, but now they were leering. The pretty view had something wrong with it, like an oceanscape rolling giddy and uncaring over stove ships and the grinning faces of men long dead. I turned up my collar against a sudden chill gust off the surface and swung back toward the house.

The maid was letting herself out the back door as I

came up the flagstone path. She had on a cloth coat and a bright knit cap with a ball on top that made her look like someone just off the boat, and she was carrying a purse the size of a steamer trunk by a strap like a tow hawser. "I'm going home now," she said. "You found Rhett?"

"Yeah."

She didn't hear me, but it must have been in my face. She looked at me closely, seemed on the edge of asking, then pulled the door shut firmly behind her and stepped off the stoop. "I'm going home now."

I watched her stumping down the driveway. At the end she turned right toward the bus stop on the corner. She didn't look back. She'd been working for the family long enough not to ask questions where Rhett was concerned. The dumb Polack bit was strictly protective coloring. What a maid knows would bring a blush to the sallow cheeks of a thirty-year man on the vice squad.

She'd locked the door, but the lock was nothing. I didn't even bother to go around to the front to see if that one was still open. I'd noticed that it was deadbolted. Curious how people, even people who are smart enough to have a lot of money, forget about things like back doors. Maybe the burglars who preyed on homes in Grosse Pointe were too classy to come in through the servants' entrance. This one wasn't. I slipped the latch almost as quickly as they do in fiction and headed up the back stairs to the smaller of the two bedrooms, which I figured was Rhett's.

The kid had his own refrigerator full of imported beer and several thousand dollars' worth of stereo equipment besides the usual bedroom stuff. No wonder he had still been living at home at an age when most people had married and moved out. I frisked the room inside out, starting with the less likely places, the way you do with the clever-clever ones. I found a stack of pornography in exquisite bindings under the bed and a crumpled pair of black bikini panties not Rhett's size behind the dresser. Too many electronic keyboards and screaming Negroes inside the album covers in the record cabinet. One of each would have been more than enough. Nothing taped behind or under drawers. Then I switched to the obvious places. He had eleven thousand dollars in cash rolled up and stashed in the toe of a bedroom slipper in the closet. Tax-free mad money from a spoiled rich kid's part-time job pushing junk. I still wasn't sure what ball I was looking for, but at least I was in the right park. The rest of the room was clean. He would be too tricky to hide his merchandise on the premises. I left the money where I'd found it and moved on to the adjoining bathroom.

It was in the medicine cabinet over the sink. After lifting things down from the glass shelves and tapping the back for hidden panels, I was replacing the items with my hand wrapped in a handkerchief to keep my prints on my fingers where they belonged when I noticed how light the can of shaving cream was. I shook it. Something bumped around inside. I pried off the top. It was a funny place to keep an address book.

The entries were in code, naturally. The last was written in a different color ink and had a hasty sort of look. I stuck the whole thing in my pocket, finished restocking the cabinet, and worked my way backward out through Rhett's room, obliterating possible prints as I

went. I snapped the latch on my way out the back door
and drove downtown and put my hat in my hand and
walked into the quiet efficiency of the Grosse Pointe
Police Station. The sergeant at the desk was polite. They
are always polite in that town. He listened to what I had
to say, then radioed the Grissoms' address to a car in
the vicinity and asked me to take a seat.

23

A CAPTAIN QUINCANNON TOOK IT. HE WAS A TALL, thin redhead leaning hard on fifty, with merry eyes and a mouth that was not merry. I didn't know him. Someday I'd meet all of them, but by that time there'd be a whole new batch coming up. His office was a pleasant carpeted oblong with a dark oak desk and baseball pictures hung on the walls. A young Quincannon grinned out at me from several of them, wearing a baggy uniform with the name of a semipro team I'd heard of once or twice on the shirt. A gold-framed triptych on the desk contained an attractive blonde in her forties and a boy and girl of about college age, both smiling the Quincannon smile. He sat me down in a comfortable chair with arms and walked around behind the desk and sat down and offered me a cigarette from a pack with some miles on it and took one for himself and used a small pair of scissors to cut it in half and put the other half back in the pack and lit up with a red plastic throwaway lighter. We blew smoke at each other's shoulder.

"You're a P.I. named Walker?" His eyes belonged to a saloon comic setting up the punch line.

"Was," I corrected. "Right now there's probably a very angry state trooper waiting for me at my office to collect my bona fides, if he hasn't already got out a BOL bulletin on me."

"Oh. You're *that* Walker."

"You've been reading the papers."

"I don't have to. You're this week's icebreaker at all the police officers' parties. Last week it was that new directive in New York calling for a cop to be read his rights and investigated every time he shoots a suspect in the line of duty."

"That bad?"

He nodded economically and went on looking at me through the smoke of his half a cigarette. "Let's have it."

"I'm working on the assumption this Paula Royce the papers have all been squawking about is still alive," I said. "She does pills, and since Rhett Grissom seems to have been the Grosse Pointe distributor for Parke-Davis, I thought he might have had recent contact with her. I went out there today to talk to him. He isn't saying much."

"We know all about Rhett Grissom. We've got an F.I. file on him as long as Woodward Avenue, but his father's money buys a lot of back-door justice. Just how were you planning to get this information out of him?"

"Not by slapping him around until the bone came through his face. I know you have to ask that question, but remember that you wouldn't be asking it at all if I didn't come here to report finding the body."

"You see a lot of the double-reverse in this work," he said dryly.

"You mean when the killer calls the cops, thinking the cops won't suspect him because he called them. That's the thinking of someone who doesn't know how cops work. But of course I might do it that way, thinking you'd think that because I know how cops work I wouldn't try a stunt like that. We can play this shell game all day and wind up where we are right now."

"It might be worth the hassle to you if you were seen coming or going."

"I talked to the maid, kind of."

He waved that away. "She's been questioned before. She hears and sees twice what she lets on, but a team of clam-crackers couldn't open her up if they worked at it a week. Tossed the house, did you?"

"I never said that. Breaking and entering isn't the way I work." There's no law against lying to a cop.

"Uh-huh." He hung on to it a moment, playing with it, then put it down. Not away. "Okay, let's just for now say that I think you're virgin. What's your interest in the Royce girl to begin with?"

"Strictly personal."

His grim mouth got grimmer. "Not good enough, Walker."

"Okay. Yesterday I had a visit from a lifetaker named Horn, Fletcher Horn, who as much as told me he's looking to shove her over. With me it's a business thing. Rumor has it I helped the girl out of the jam she was in with the law. Whether it's true or not doesn't matter. If I ever get back my license it would be nice if a potential client didn't have to wonder about the services of a private investigator that got another client killed. Twice.''

"Better. Paula Royce was your client, then?"

"You're putting words in my mouth again, Captain. A client is someone I agree to represent. Money doesn't have to change hands for the definition to hold, although it's nicer when it does. The word's abroad that I helped her. I'm stuck with it either way."

"You split the hair plenty fine, I'll say that for you." He smudged out his butt in one of those beaten tin ashtrays kids make in shop for their fathers. It looked as if he'd been using it awhile. "What makes her still alive?"

"For one thing, the number of people who want me to think she isn't. For another, the fact that no one connected with the Iroquois Heights Police bothered to go over and identify her body."

"Oh them."

"Yeah," I said, "but they're still cops. They don't usually leave any *t*'s uncrossed unless someone makes it worth their while not to cross them."

"Pretty thin."

"Fat leads are a rare animal in my part of the forest."

"Mine too. Would this Horn be someone who would be likely to knock around a scroat like Rhett Grissom for the girl's whereabouts?"

"He would be someone who would be very likely to do just that. He's proud of his ability to kill without weapons."

"Tell me more about this charming fellow."

I looked at my cigarette. "What I know is third-hand and sketchy. He just did three out of five at state for Grand Theft Auto, but that may have been his idea because he was hot. The reason he was hot is he'd just cooled a grand jury witness right under the cops' noses. Word is he's working for the Colombians at present, who are moving or have moved in on the area drug trade. Under another name, Paula Royce testified against their associates down in Florida a while back and did some damage. They're looking for reparations.'' I described Horn as well as I could, dwelling on his small hands and feet.

"Sketchy, huh? What do you call a detailed report?" He was suspicious. They always are when the job looks too easy.

"He likes to talk. And I've been in my line a long time. I have sources."

"I'll bet. Must be nice knowing you can knock heads without the press and the politicians and the A.C.L.U. breathing down your neck."

"I'm just a private agent, Captain, or I was. I have to cut corners somewhere. They don't turn to water when they get a hinge at my ID like they do with yours."

"Greener grass, Walker." He planted his hands on the arms of his swivel. "You don't have to deal every day with the hard-gloss punks they grow up here like I do. Mention prison and they laugh in your face. Juvenile hall is paved slick as spit with their fathers' money. They slide out faster than they slide in. Scratch Rhett Grissom and make room for two more half his age with twice his smarts. We're spinning our wheels on a glass highway up here."

"Beats rolling backward."

"We do our share of that too." He got up and stuck out his hand. "Appreciate your coming down. We'll tap the warden's office in Jackson for the file on Horn and have his picture out on a circular this afternoon. I'm turning you over to Sergeant Minch to get all this down on paper. He's our fastest typist. We'll have you out of here in half an hour. Don't forget where we are next time something comes up."

I rose and grasped the hand, which felt as if it belonged around the neck of a baseball bat. He was six-two and hard as a pine board. "Thanks, Captain. I'm not used to courtesy in a police station. A skipper like you could give the business a bad name."

"I'm not tough. I hung all that up with the uniform."

"Like hell you're not tough."

His smile was economical, but a ghost of the young athlete's grin waltzed around the edges. "Stay in touch."

By the time I got away from Sergeant Minch and his magic typewriter I had a ticket on my windshield for parking in a police zone. I considered going back in and paying it, but there were no other spaces in sight and I'd just find another ticket waiting for me when I returned. So I climbed behind the wheel and reached across and opened the glove compartment to put it away. A hand grenade plopped out and rolled across the floor toward me, wobbling drunkenly.

24

"Thanks, Tim."

The red-haired captain cradled the receiver and looked at me. "That was Officer Drinkwater calling from Belle Isle. The Detroit bomb squad has officially declared your pineapple a dud."

"I figured as much or there'd be a black smudge on the street out front where my car is parked." I was burning my fourth Winston since returning to his office and waiting for the mud and loose asphalt to dry on my suit before brushing it off. I'd done some rolling on the pavement after the grenade showed up. "All I needed to round out this case was a killer with a sense of humor."

"You're sure it was Horn planted it?"

"I have to be. If I thought there were two like him kicking around I'd deliver my license to the state cops in person and take up making lamps out of old Buick engine blocks. Besides, demolitions are among his specialties. I figure this was a friendly warning for me to take a hike. I get them now and then, though they're seldom this articulate."

"He wouldn't have the brass to plant it while you were parked in front of a police station."

"He would if I were using J. Edgar Hoover as a hood ornament. You've never met him." I killed the stub in the homemade ashtray. "But he'd have to have been hanging around the Grissom place until I showed and then followed me here, which is less than likely. He could have done it anytime after our little meeting in my office."

"I guess warnings like this roll right off hard guys like you," he said dryly.

"He scares the hell out of me, Captain. That could just as well have been the real thing, and I've seen what they can do in close quarters. He knew that, which is why he made that choice. His hobby is psychology."

Quincannon poked at the sorry pack of cigarettes on his desk without taking one. "He ought to turn it on himself. No sane man does what he did to Rhett Grissom."

"Prison's lifted the lid off steadier guys than him."

He said, "I'll have Minch type up the report on your little post-Christmas surprise package."

"You know the details." I stood and reached for the doorknob. "Thanks again, Captain. I bet you were something to see out on the diamond."

He reminded me to pay my ticket and get my car the hell out of the blue zone.

THE OTHER SIDE OF THE COIN WAS WAITING IN MY LIT-tle reception room when I got back. As I entered, a square-jawed number in a regulation haircut and a blue suit under a black coat got up from the bench. He was as tall as the captain in Grosse Pointe and his gaze was blue and direct.

"Amos Walker?"

I said, "Isn't he in yet? I want to hire him to follow my wife. She's got Motel Back like Yvonne Goolagong's got tennis elbow."

"Nice try, Walker. I've seen your picture." He flashed his badge and ID folder. "Officer Tynan, State Police. I was here earlier. You weren't. I was going to give you another ten minutes and then swear out a warrant. I think you know what I'm here for."

"A Captain Quincannon of the Grosse Pointe Police wanted me even more than you did. Let's do it."

Maintenance had been busy. The office door had been removed and the broken glass swept up. Tynan didn't comment on the missing door. He was the kind of cop that wears a shoulder holster to the beach. In a couple of years he'd be a lieutenant. I flipped my license photostat and gun permit onto the desk in front of him and took the original license down from the wall and out of its frame and added it to the pile. He gathered up the talismans that kept me eating and cut out without so much as a click of his heels. No broken saber, no Rogue's March, nothing. There's no romance left in the world.

I locked the outer door behind him and went back in and shucked my outerwear and sat behind the desk to scowl at Rhett Grissom's address book. It didn't look like much of a code. Numbers instead of letters and vice versa. I hesitated with my hand on the drawer handle, then opened it and got out a pencil and paper. I couldn't live my life looking under the bed for hand grenades.

The telephone interrupted me twenty minutes in. It was Theodore Grundy of the Justice Department.

"I've spoken with my superiors," he said.

"Yeah," I said. "There's been a new development in the case." I told him about Grissom. I didn't mention the book.

A moment of silence for the dear departed. Then: "You think Horn killed him?"

"Somebody had to. Why not Horn?"

He paused. "You really don't know where Paula Royce is, do you?"

"I don't. Don't as in 'do not.' Do not as in the opposite of do. Grundy, I don't."

He believed me then. For some reason I thought he never would. "I'll get back to you in five minutes." He broke off.

It was closer to ten. "Yeah, Grundy," I said into the mouthpiece.

"The offer stands, Walker. We can't have too many investigators cluttering up the landscape. There's talk of the FBI getting involved, and even the Federal Bureau of Narcotics. I've got the go-ahead to swing your license for you if you'll agree to forget all about Paula Royce."

"Sorry."

Pause. "What's that mean? I thought that's what you wanted."

"It is. But it has to be on my terms, not yours. Otherwise having a license doesn't mean anything. It's a little thing called holding up my end of a bargain. I wouldn't expect you to understand that, working for the government.''

''That's twice you've said that. I resent it twice as much this time. My integrity—''

''Is so lightweight it moves with the tide. Good-bye, Grundy. So glad you called.''

''Listen, Walk—'' The rest of it got trapped in the wires.

The telephone rang again after a few seconds. I let it. It stopped at eight.

The code was nothing. I broke it in less than an hour. The numbers ran backward up the alphabet from Z starting with 3, skipping every fifth digit. I recognized some of the names of customers on Grissom's list and was surprised by one or two, although there was no reason I should have been, given the times. My interest was in the hurried last entry, but it was a disappointment. The name was F. Esterhazy, the number Fern's new address in Grosse Pointe.

She'd lied to me about not using pills between parties, but I get lied to a lot, and it slides off me like tobacco juice off polished brass. If she was a regular customer— and a quick look through the rest of the book would establish that—it was only natural that a new entry would be made for her after her move from home. I pushed the book away in disgust and fumbled for a cigarette.

I didn't light it. Two memories shoved me, then scampered away, whispering to each other and giggling. Something Fern had said in The Chord Progression that strange Christmas Eve. Something else Gable Reinhardt, Barry Stackpole's research assistant, had said in the Sextant Bar. Just two things told me by two not very different people on either side of a murder. I unlocked my little book of dynamite from the file cabinet and called the number listed there of a guy in records at the City-County Building who owed me.

When I finished talking to him, I got my .38 out of the drawer and snapped the holster onto my belt. What I could get for wearing it on the street without a permit was a lot better than what I'd get if I didn't.

A CLOUD BANK WAS BACKING IN FROM THE NORTH LIKE a fat headwaiter leaving a big tipper's table, but there was still no snow. Winter without snow is always holding its breath. The air smells of iron and the streets have a bleak empty look. Everybody watches the sky. It's like the interval between the time they come for your cellmate and when you hear the ragged shots of the firing squad outside, and the silence screws down tighter and tighter until the volley when it comes is like an orgasm.

The tenants' lot behind Fern's building was filled, so I parked on the street and climbed the stairs to her apartment. She answered the buzzer almost before I could take my finger off the button. She was wearing a clinging green skirt, platforms, and an ivory-colored blouse unbuttoned just one button past far enough. She started a little when she recognized me, but she covered up nicely.

"Well, well," she said. "Door-to-door shamus."

"I bet you worked a week on that one. Am I welcome inside or are you curling your eyelashes?"

"Inside what?" Her tone was husky. But she made

room for me, just enough so that I brushed her breasts coming in.

I pointed at them. "I hope those are registered."

"You should know." She closed the door and leaned back against it, vamp style.

I walked around the acre of living room, opened the door to the study and looked in, glanced down the hallway opposite. I'd have had to pack a lunch before searching the whole apartment.

"Looking for a way out so soon?"

She didn't sound nervous. But then she'd had two husbands and a lot of walk-ons to test her acting. I turned around and almost bumped into her. She snaked her arms inside my coat and pressed a hand against the small of my back. I curled an arm behind her out of reflex. She leaned back against it. Her long thick red hair tickled my wrist. The musk was strong today.

"I missed this," she murmured. "Most of the men I go out with are a foot short or else they tower over me and we have to find a cab with a sun roof for them to stick their heads through like giraffes. Kiss me."

I obliged. When our lips were almost touching I said, "Rhett Grissom's dead."

Her eyes opened. The raw silver in them shone. We were so close I could focus on only one at a time. "What?" She whispered it.

"Your first husband beat him to death," I said.

25

I DON'T KNOW HOW LONG WE STAYED LIKE THAT. Probably only a few seconds before she disentangled herself. "Have you been drinking? My first husband is—"

"He's out. They let him out Christmas Day. Just in time for him to strangle Moses True. He's been one busy ex-con."

She glared at me but said nothing. She moved a little toward the inlaid table near one modular sofa. I kept on.

"You talked too much Christmas Eve, but then you'd been sucking up pills and gin all night and were wearing a cloud for a hat. You told me he was pulling three to five in Jackson for stealing a car. Horn said yesterday he just got off three years of a nickel stretch in Jackson. Someone else said he was inside for Grand Theft Auto. But a lot has happened lately, and I wouldn't have put them together if I hadn't seen your name on Rhett Grissom's list of customers. I checked with records and learned that Fern Esterhazy and Fletcher Horn were married in Detroit three years ago, and divorced a couple of months later. That would have been after he was arrested and sentenced." I paused for breath. "Where's Paula Royce?"

"In a Canadian morgue." She kept drifting toward the table, her eyes on me. It had a small drawer in the side. "Okay, I married a crook and a killer. I fixed that mistake. How do you get from that to Paula Royce?"

"It's not that much of a jump. She needs her drugs more than you. She's smart, but that kind of need goes past brains. She got in touch with Grissom and gave him this address for delivery. You don't come out of this end looking so bad, really. If Horn knew you were hiding her he wouldn't have had to beat it out of Grissom."

"He knows?" For a moment she stopped drifting. The skin of her face was drawn tight.

"He knew as much about Paula's habit as I did. He knew that if she was still in the area she'd make contact with Grissom sometime. Horn was just guessing she was back from Canada. So was I, but I knew she'd be hiding somewhere waiting for Arthur Stillson to get back from the Bahamas and provide her with the phony identification she needed to get shed of Paula Royce. But I have to wonder why she was hiding here specifically. For that I have to go back to Christmas Eve again, the night someone killed Bud Broderick in Iroquois Heights. Stay away from that drawer."

She dived for it. I grabbed her wrist and twisted it and jerked open the drawer with my other hand. A .32 Browning automatic lay inside. She clawed for it with her free hand. I twisted harder and she squealed. I snatched up the gun.

205

Maintaining my grip, I backwalked her to the sofa and pushed her roughly. The backs of her knees hit the edge of the seat and she collapsed into it. Then she broke. Sobs shook her body. She hugged herself and leaned forward, her hair tumbling in front of her face and completely hiding it.

"Paula knew you'd provide her with a safe house while she was waiting," I said. I was still holding the automatic. "She wasn't aware of your connection with the man who was out to kill her, or she wouldn't have taken that risk. But she was counting on you. You said yourself you weren't close friends. Why, then? Because she had something on you.

"Last time I was here I asked you why you picked me to spend Christmas Eve with when you had a wide field of eligible men to choose from. God knows my manly good looks are hard to pass up, but those aren't what you look for. I wasn't as old or anywhere near as rich as the kind you prefer. But I was something none of the others were. I was a detective, and therefore the best possible alibi."

She'd stopped sobbing. I couldn't see her eyes, but I knew she was watching me through the veil of her hair. I realized then that I still had the pistol and dropped it into my coat pocket. I don't like to wave around strange guns.

I said, "Unless they get a corpse when it's still warm, medical examiners can't tell within a couple of hours when death occurred. Having been the wife of a killer you might know that. What better way to account for your whereabouts on the night Bud died than to be able to point to a sort of detective? It was just extra insurance, because there was only one other person who could place you at Paula Royce's house that night, and you thought she was too zonked out to remember. Hell, she might even think she did it herself. Only she didn't. When the pills wore off she remembered just enough to use that knowledge against you for refuge. Why'd you kill him, Fern?''

''You don't know that I did it. You're just trying to talk yourself back into a job.'' She scooped her hair back behind her shoulders with both hands, like an explorer parting brush. Her face was bone-white except for her eyes and the end of her nose. They were almost, but not quite, as red as spilled blood. Nothing is that red. ''My father can fix that for you. It'll save him the trouble of having to sue you for slander later on. Shall I call him?''

I grinned. ''Everybody's trying to give me back my license. What was it with Bud, a sibling thing? That happens in families where a youngster's used to being an only child. It gets ugly when an inheritance is involved.''

''It was an accident.''

This was a new voice. Shoving aside my coattails to get at the Smith & Wesson, I swung toward the hallway to the right. I hesitated, then dropped my hand from the butt. She'd gotten rid of the bangs and dyed her hair dark blond, but you can't do much about eyes and complexion. She had on a yellow-and-white-striped blouse and a brown flaring skirt and she was barefoot, as she'd been when I first saw her, somewhere on the other side of the last ice age. Ten days ago.

I drew a deep breath and let it out slowly. Somehow

I'd hoped I was wrong about the whole thing. She was looking at me.

"I don't remember much from that evening," she said, "but I do remember that I woke up hearing voices and came into the kitchen as they were struggling for the gun. It was in Bud's hand. Then it went off. Twice. Like that." She clapped her hands twice fast. "It sounded almost like one shot."

"You're the prime suspect, and a junkie to boot," Fern spat. "Who's going to believe you in a town my father owns down to the fire hydrants?"

"I will." I was looking at Paula. "Keep going."

"There was a lot of blood." She spoke slowly and distinctly, like someone remembering a past life under hypnosis. "Bud just seemed to hang there a long time, but I suppose it was only a second or two. Then he sagged against Fern. She screamed and jumped back and he fell." She paused, appeared to lose the thread. "Poor Bud. I had too many pills one night and told him too much about myself. Protecting me made him feel like a man. His mother never gave him that chance.

"I guess I fainted then, because I don't remember anything until I woke up on the floor. Bud was lying where he'd fallen. Fern was gone. I just knew I had to get out of there. I'd been involved in one murder case already, and there were people who would kill me if it got out who I was. That's why I came to you."

"Thanks."

She smiled then, faintly. "I heard about what happened. I never asked you to go to jail for me. If I'd thought for one minute that you would—"

"You'd have done just what you did," I finished.

"Everyone uses me; that's what I'm here for. Everyone has the right to save his own skin his own way. The press made out like I was protecting a client. I let them. That kind of publicity is good for business, if I ever get my business back. Truth is I don't like Cecil Fish or his pet cops and I let them get to me. I like to call it principles. Some might call it plain muleheadedness. They're entitled to their opinion. How come me and not the Justice Department?"

"You know about that?" Her eyes widened a little, then went back to normal. "Stupid. Of course you do, or you wouldn't be here. I tried the number they gave me for emergencies. No one answered. Then I saw your card next to the phone. There was no one else."

"What was so special about Canada? I could have driven you to Metro and seen you off for anywhere."

"The people who want me dead spend a lot of time around airports. I couldn't risk being recognized. For some time I've kept an apartment in Toronto for just this sort of emergency. It was the key to that apartment I showed you, and said it belonged to a fishing cabin owned by Bud's stepfather to cover my tracks. But the story was as big in Canada as it was here. I kept trying that number until I reached someone from the Justice Department. I told him I was across the border, but I didn't say where; I'd already trusted one person more than I like. He said he'd see what kind of deal could be struck with the Canadian authorities and told me to stay in touch. Now that everyone thought I was dead I was safe from the police here, and I remembered what you'd said about the lawyer in Iroquois Heights who could fix me up with new identification. But he wasn't in. I had to have someplace to stay while I was waiting. A motel or hotel was too risky; too many people moving in and out. I called Fern's parents' house, disguising my voice, and they gave me this address.''

''Sorry I missed that meeting,'' I said, and looked at Fern. ''What happened Christmas Eve?''

She'd had time to collect herself. Casually she fitted a cigarette into an Aqua-filter and lit it with a gold lighter no thicker than a quarter, tipped back her head and squirted smoke at the ceiling. The theatrics of dancing with lung cancer. She crossed her long legs and said nothing.

I nodded. ''If I have to carry it I will. The Colombians stumbled on Paula by accident. Maybe one of them accompanied Moses True on his rounds and happened to spot her arriving for one of these dope parties that are so hard to stay away from. They wanted very badly to finish their business with her for what she had done to their organization in Miami, but they were getting conservative and they didn't want to attract any more headlines than they already had getting settled in Detroit. So they did some digging and found out that a reliable lifetaker was about to be sprung from stir, one who knew the area and who had never been legally linked to a homicide. Then they did some more digging and found you, his ex-wife, traveling in the same circles as Paula. What were you, the spotter?''

She didn't answer. She didn't have to. She puffed on the cigarette and took it out of her mouth, clicking her long red nails like castinets and staring directly into my collarbone. I might not have been right on track, but I hadn't lost sight of the rails yet. I chugged on.

"My guess is they threatened you with your first husband. It can be done. He scares me, and I've met my share of killers. Faced with that threat, you agreed to keep tabs on her during Horn's final weeks of imprisonment and make sure she stayed put until he was available. What went wrong was you made the mistake of taking Stepbrother Bud along on one of these partygoing reconnaissance missions, where he fell hard for the mark. Sticky, but still not disastrous. Until he decided to move in with her."

I stopped talking. Fern was looking at me now. The skin of her face was so tight I could trace the outlines of her skull.

"I loved him," she said.

26

THE AIR WAS AS BRITTLE AS OLD BONE. WE KEPT PO-
sition like three dowagers posing for an antique camera.
Even the smoke from Fern's cigarette hung motionless.

"You were trying to get Bud out of there that night,"
I prompted.

"Yes." She breathed some of the dry air. "He never
loved Paula. He knew she was in some kind of danger
and protecting her made him feel grown up. Like with
you. That's the secret of her appeal, that phony helpless
act she puts on.

"Horn was getting out Christmas Day. Bud was no
match for him. I haven't met anyone yet who is. He
would've squashed Bud like an ant just to avoid having
to step around him. Bud wouldn't believe me when I
told him. He'd only met Horn at my wedding, and he
had no idea what he was like. Bud was only seventeen
years old then. So I told him the whole story, how I
was fingering Paula for the Colombians because my first
husband would kill me otherwise. He called me a murderous bitch and told me to get out. When I wouldn't,

he got Paula's gun and said he'd shoot me if I didn't leave. I was half-crazy. I couldn't talk to him with that gun in his hand, so I tried to take it away from him.'' Her mouth worked some more, but no words came out. She took a drag, but the smoke went down the wrong way and she started hacking bitterly. The hacking turned to sobbing. If it was an act it was a good one.

''Paula told me you were really a nice girl,'' I said. ''That used to mean a woman who could love a man in spite of what he didn't have. I guess you fit that definition. You worked overtime hiding it. Maybe you have to in your set.''

''Amos, I can't stay here,'' said Paula. Her face was pale under the South American coloring. ''If Horn knows where I am he's on his way here now.''

''He'd be here already if he knew. Grissom probably told him you were at Fern Esterhazy's place.''

Fern stood. Her eyes were swollen now. ''Horn would think that meant Father's house. I moved here to stay away from that killer.''

''He'll find out. If not from your father and stepmother, from someone else. With any luck we'll have some law here by that time.'' I took the automatic out of my pocket and laid it on the telephone table to dial.

''No! Call this number.'' Paula drew a dog-eared card with a telephone number scribbled on the back from her brassiere and held it out.

''Not the Justice Department,'' I said. ''They have to have your bust measurement down in triplicate before they send out an agent. Give me a cop who can't spell cat anytime.''

I told Fern to sit down and kept my eyes on her while

I spoke to two officers to get where I was going. Finally the familiar busted-windpipe voice came on the wire.

"If you're looking for a job, Walker, we're fresh out of openings on the custodial staff. We'll always be fresh out when you call."

"Nothing of the sort, Proust," I said. "I just called to ask if you thought we might have snow for New Year's Day and if you might be interested in withdrawing the charges against my license if I hand you Bud Broderick's murderer."

"Haven't they buried her yet?" He sounded pleased with his wit.

"If you mean Paula Royce, there's a law against burying women alive in this state. I'm standing across from her right now."

A swivel chair squealed miles away. "Shoot it to me." He wasn't pleased now.

"She's not the one you want anyway. She never was, but you wouldn't have cared about that, which is why she didn't have to look too far to find someone to get her to Canada. The killer is also in the room. Now if you and Cecil Fish want me to go to the press with the girl whose death you both confirmed, we will have some cameras. I just thought you might like to be able to throw the real culprit at the folks who ask what about Paula Royce. But I'm often wrong. So long, Proust." I started to hang up.

"Walker? Walker!"

I put the receiver back to my ear. "Yeah."

There was a muffled noise on the other end, as of someone talking to someone else with a hand over the mouthpiece.

"Proust?"

"Okay, Walker, deal. If what you got is good enough."

"I think you'll agree it is." I gave him the address in Grosse Pointe.

"That's out of our jurisdiction."

"I know. I'm calling the G.P.P.D. next. You might call them too and let them know you're coming. Send Bloodworth. If Zorn wants to come along he can, but if he messes the rug, out he goes."

"They're on their way, fucker. Ten minutes. And Walker?"

"Yeah."

"If this turns out to be nothing I'll nail your balls over my office door."

"Colorful, Proust. But not original."

He made a rude noise and rang off.

Next I called the Grosse Pointe cops and talked to Captain Quincannon.

"I don't want those crooked bastards in my yard," he said coldly, after I'd filled him in.

I said, "They're not all crooked, Captain. And this did start out to be their case."

"Working a deal, are you?"

"I have to eat."

"I heard it before. Be there in five."

Paula was glaring at me when I put down the instrument. "Pretty slick."

"If I were that I would have stayed in the army and been a lieutenant colonel by now."

"Is that true what you said about helping me because you thought I was innocent?"

215

"Me lie to a cop?"

"That doesn't explain why you didn't let me go to jail while you investigated the murder."

"You said yourself I'd promised to help."

"And you said that wasn't meant to be a blank check."

"You I lied to."

She was watching me with a look I've seen a couple of times, too far apart. "I don't think I ever knew anyone like you," she said.

"There used to be a lot of us."

I was still watching Fern. She was slumped on the sofa, one arm dangling over the edge, knees sprawled apart. She looked like something wrung out and flung into a corner. A fresh cigarette smoked untended in an ashtray on the end table. I walked over and put it out. I'm a compulsive or I wouldn't have done that and left her gun lying next to the telephone. I might as well have chucked it out the window and thrown myself after it. When I turned around at Paula's gasp, Horn was smiling at me from the apartment doorway.

27

"Go ahead," he said.

He stood just inside the threshold, just a large mild-looking fattish man in the same blue suit and gray coat he'd been wearing when I met him. His hands were at his sides and one of the coat sleeves that were too long for his short arms hung down over the bandage on his wrist, concealing it. With his enormous chest and broad face he looked like a professional wrestler who had retired and gone to work in the front office.

He'd followed my eyes to the gun on the table. I was ten feet closer to it than he was, just a step and a scoop away, but I didn't try for it. "I'll pass," I told him. "I've seen you move." I didn't mention the revolver behind my hip. He was too fast even for that.

Something like disappointment fluttered over his fair features, but he covered up well. His friendly eyes moved to the woman on the sofa. "Hello, Fern."

Fern didn't respond. She was sitting up straight now, her hands braced on the cushions. Her breathing was audible.

Paula stood in the middle of the room with her back to the casement window. She'd guessed the newcomer's identity, but you'd have to have seen her in various situations to realize that. A slight whitening around the nostrils, flesh pulled taut and shiny across cheeks and forehead. But for that she might have been waiting for a bus.

Fear crept into the room like cold through an open window.

Horn closed the door behind him without turning around. His slightest movements were hypnotic. They had the velvet-wrapped power of a bear pacing its cage.

He was still looking at Fern. "I spoke to your step-mother over the phone. She wouldn't tell me where you'd moved, so I went out there and talked to the neighbors. I told them I was your second husband's law-yer and that I had to have your signature on some pa-pers. Somebody remembered the name printed on the moving van. I called the company and they gave me this address. You're a lot short of smart, Fern. Miles short."

"I had to do it." She spoke rapidly. "She said if I didn't take her in she'd tell what happened Christmas Eve. I was going to call you, Fletcher."

"No, you weren't. Her body in your apartment would have been harder to explain. Besides, you're afraid of me."

She forced her mouth into a pleasant expression, got up, started snaking toward him in a jerky parody of her usual style. She put her arms around his neck. He was an inch taller. She kissed him lingeringly. I worked a hand inside my coat and around behind.

"Still think I'm afraid?" she asked him, coming up.

Horn hadn't moved. He was wearing the same tight-lipped smile he'd had on when he came in. He reached up and grasped her wrists in both hands. She took in her breath. I knew that hold. He brought his hands down and out to the sides, twisting her elbows in. She sank to her knees, whimpering.

"You should've just done your part and backed out." His tone betrayed all the effort of a fat dog snoozing in the shade. "Now I'll have to mop up, and you know how I hate working for free."

"Let her go, Horn."

He looked at me, then at the .38 in my hand. His smile may have flickered a little. He relaxed his grip. Fern folded the rest of the way to the floor and lay in a heap of red hair and long legs at his feet. She was sobbing for real now.

Horn said, "I still got rust in my joints or that wouldn't have happened. I was counting on that present I left you in your car to keep you from getting tangled up in my feet. You want my hands up or what? I'm unarmed."

"You're never that. Fold them across your chest."

He obliged. It seemed to amuse him.

"Let's talk," I said. "Why'd you kill Moses True?"

"I never said I did."

"We'll pretend."

"He was trying to chew both ends of the string. He found out where Paula Royce lived and offered to sell the address to my employers. They laughed at him and said they could find that out without his help. Then he threatened to go to the cops if they didn't pay him off. They paid him off."

"Why'd you strangle him?"

"The day I need anything more than my hands to cool a dud like True is the day I retire. The same goes for his fucking dogs."

"Today's the day. What about Rhett Grissom? He gave you the information you were after or you wouldn't be here. He wasn't the kind to hold out so long you had to beat him to death."

"We're just pretending, remember. I said I was rusty. I forgot to pull my punches."

"I think it's more than that. I think you slipped your cog. Get out of here," I told Paula.

She stayed put. I said it again, and then she started hesitantly toward the door. I glanced at her and away from Horn, which was my second big mistake that day. When I looked back he was moving.

He caught my gun hand with the side of his foot just as my finger pulsed on the trigger. The report gulped up all the sound in the room. Something shattered, the noise falling tinnily on my battered eardrums. Horn pivoted clear around on the other foot and kicked me in the ribs. My coat saved them from breakage, but my lungs turned inside out and I staggered. Before I could catch my balance, the edge of a stiffened hand came down on my forearm and I wasn't holding the gun any longer. I had True's mongrel to thank for his not having broken my arm; it obviously hurt him to use that hand. Lucky me.

I hadn't fought straight karate style since my M.P. training, and no one had been out to kill anyone that time. But instinct is a powerful weapon. Instead of re-sisting I went with the blow, spinning on the ball of my left foot and slicing the stiffened fingers of my right hand into where his solar plexus would have been had he cooperated. He twisted just in time for me to graze his rib cage instead. I was rewarded with a loud grunt and a whoosh of spent breath. I jabbed at his eyes with my other hand. He ducked and shouldered me low in the abdomen, tearing me off my feet. My elbow struck the floor and my arm went numb. I tried to roll, but he was on top of me too quickly. Fingers closed around my throat.

Over his beefy shoulder I glimpsed a flash of red hair, and then Fern was gone out the door. I decided I didn't blame her. Then I forgot about her. Horn's breath hissed through his teeth, flecking my face with spittle. He was the only one of us who was breathing. I rabbit-punched him behind the ear as hard as I had ever hit anyone or anything. All I did was hurt my hand. My vision turned black around the edges.

A fresh explosion rocked the room. An astonished "Huh!" broke from Horn, and his weight sagged. His grip on my throat went slack. Sweet air poured down into my lungs. Paula's face hovered somewhere over-head, behind the smoking blue mouth of the .32 auto-matic thrust out in front of her in both hands. Her eyes were very large.

I was starting to push out from under the limp sack of meat when it went rigid, and then Horn was up on one knee and pivoting. I shouted a warning. It came out a strangled croak. Before Paula could move, he swept a hand around and grasped the gun by its barrel and twisted. The muzzle spat red and blue fire. Out of the corner of my eye I saw the casement window collapse in a slow-motion shower of glittering iridescence, all in eerie silence because I was still deafened by the earlier blast. The gun came free as Horn rose and backhanded Paula with his empty hand. She spun and collided with the telephone table, overturning it and sending Ma Bell's instrument flying. I got a hand under me to push myself up.

"Horn!"

The amplified address squeezed past the ringing in my ears. It must have been nearly as loud as the shots. Horn froze. He was holding the automatic by its butt now, standing halfway between me on the floor and the girl half-reclining on the dislodged table and the debris that had scattered when it fell.

"Horn!" repeated the deep voice. "This is the police. All the exits are covered. Throw out your weapon and come out with your hands on top of your head or we'll open fire."

I started to get up. Horn switched hands on the gun and covered me. "You stay there!"

I sank back down on one hip. My breath was rasping in my throat. Horn reached down and grabbed Paula's arm and yanked her stumbling to her feet. She was still trying to catch her balance when he flung an arm around her neck and propelled her toward the open door that led to the stairs. His right side under the coat was slick with blood where the bullet from the .32 had grazed him.

"I got a woman hostage here!" he shouted. "Anyone gets near me I blow her backbone out her belly." He jammed the gun into her ribs and twisted it until she squealed.

There was a short silence. Then:

"What do you want, Horn?" The voice sounded weary and vaguely familiar over the bullhorn. My ears were beginning to open up. The voice belonged to Captain Quincannon.

The killer chortled. "That's better. I want all you cops to clear out. Out of the building, off the street. I got a nice new car parked down the block. I see a uniform or anyone who looks like he's someone who might be a cop on my way there, it'll be just too bad for the woman. Got that?" Another pause. "I said, 'Got that?' "

"Can't do it. Why don't you just give yourself up and save us the trouble of shooting you?"

"I'm not in the business of saving cops trouble! You want raw meat? We deliver. I got nothing to lose."

"He means it, Captain," I called.

"Walker? That you?"

I said it was. "Horn's a professional. Pros don't have to bluff."

Silence again. Quincannon broke it, without the bullhorn this time.

"You win, Horn. Give us ten minutes to clear the street."

"You got five!" He winked at me. "You and me next time."

I said nothing.

A general rustle of movement floated up the stairs. Horn nudged the door farther open with the end of his gun to watch down the stairwell, holding Paula in front of him.

I glanced around the room quickly. My revolver had come to rest against the base of the stereo cabinet. Well, it was the next logical step, logic being what it had been lately. I took a breath and rolled.

Horn shouted and fired. I didn't bother to see where the bullet went. It didn't hit me, anyway. I fell on top of the .38 and scrambled to get it and me into position. While I was doing all this I was dead five times. But Paula was struggling to get loose, kicking him in the shins with her bare heels and jostling his gun arm. I shot him under that arm. At that instant, several guns rattle-banged in jackhammer succession, punctuated by the shuddery boom of a shotgun going off in close quarters. Horn slammed backward against the door casing and slid down spraddle-legged. He sat on the floor with his chin in his throat and most of his chest gone.

Munchkin voices yammered hysterically under the echo of the blast. It was the telephone alarm, telling us the receiver was off the hook.

Dick Bloodworth came to the door cradling a riot gun that went like hell with his jacket and tie. Blue smoke curled up the stairwell and parted around him. His eyes lighted on Horn just long enough to determine he wasn't worth looking at, then went to the pale-faced girl leaning against the edge of the door, and finally to me. I was still kneeling on the floor with the gun dangling between my palms.

"You should've done your praying when it counted." He tried to sound bantering and came up yards short. His face was gray under the pigment.

"I did." I got up, holstering the .38. "He isn't the one I called Proust about. She flew the coop."

224

"If you mean the tall redhead," said Captain Quincannon from the staircase landing, "we got her downstairs. She was coming out as we were coming in."

"She's Fern Esterhazy, Charles Esterhazy's daughter. She killed Bud Broderick." I paused. "Meet Paula Royce, the only one in this room who never killed anybody."

They looked at her with new interest but said nothing. Some uniforms were on the landing behind Quincannon and Bloodworth, murmuring among themselves and gaping at the corpse on the threshold. Sergeant Zorn, wearing his overcoat and jaunty fur hat with feather, elbowed his way through and whistled. "Looks like he bought the full load."

Bloodworth was starting to feel the impact. "He called it. Why don't they just let us do our job without killing them?"

"The hell with him and everyone like him." I righted the overturned table and put the telephone on top of it and thumbed down the plunger, releasing it for the dial tone. Then I turned to Paula. "Where's that card with Uncle Sam's number?"

Outside, an ambulance wheeled whooping into our street.

28

ANOTHER NEW YEAR'S EVE AT THE END OF ANOTHER year. The temperature had dropped fourteen degrees since noon and the National Weather Service had issued a travelers' advisory for all of southeastern Michigan, predicting eight to ten inches of snow by morning. The police were broadcasting huffy warnings to partygoers: "Space out your drinks before hitting the road or see in the new year behind bars." The spirit of brotherhood was already fraying around the edges.

I emptied my Christmas bottle into a pony glass and sat down in front of the stereo, considering Ella Fitzgerald's invitation to follow her and climb the stairs to where love was for sale. She would find me lousy company. My muscles ached and it hurt to swallow. After three days I could still feel Horn's fingers on my throat.

I had spent the better part of two of those days driving back and forth between two police departments, giving the same story to bored sergeants seated at antique typewriters. At least they gave me coffee in Grosse Pointe. In the Heights I got blamed for screwing up the year-end crime statistics and I could dry up and blow away for all they gave a damn. Cecil Fish was especially grumpy because the incumbent whose state senate seat he was after had announced shortly after Christmas that he had decided to run again after all. So in Iroquois Heights they gave me to a cop who was deaf in one ear and typed with one finger.

I never saw any of them again, except of course the cops and Sandy Broderick, who got his network spot. A son killed being chivalrous swung a big club in the Nielsens.

The telephone interrupted Ella while she was peddling old love and new love and everything but true love. I turned down the volume and answered.

"Thought you bachelor types were all out partying," Dick Bloodworth's voice announced.

I set down my glass. "No you didn't, or you wouldn't have called. Where are you?"

"Station, where else? I pulled night watch, what else? I thought you might like to know; Fish is holding Paula Royce as a material witness in the Broderick case. She's got more guards on her than Fern Esterhazy had up at County before her old man bailed her yesterday."

"She's out and Paula's in. There's a moral under there someplace, but I'm too sore to dig it up." I breathed some air. "It seems to me that witness Horn smoked was under heavy guard too."

"Thank God there aren't many like him."

"One was too much," I said. "And you know damn well there are getting to be more just like him all the time. What happens after the trial? To Paula, I mean."

"That's the feds' headache. New name, new place, I

227

guess. Until someone recognizes her again. Those Colombians put on a lot of miles.''

''I never got around to thanking her. She had a chance to rabbit when Horn and I were scuffling, but she gave it up to save my hide.''

''It evens out. You saved hers. Besides, you'll get your chance when Fish subpoenas you to testify.''

''Like hell. He'll jerk her in and out of the courtroom like a piece of chicken in a four-bit pot of soup and I'll still be sitting there with my mouth open when she's gone.''

''Yeah, well.'' His tone lightened. ''I hear you're getting your ticket back.''

''By slow freight. Proust's a man of his word when you get one out of him that doesn't have just four letters in it, but he's not fond of my guts. I'll be back in harness by Groundhog Day if he doesn't decide to take a vacation first.'' I wet my lips on the edge of my glass. The stuff tasted like sour grapes. ''How's the cop business?''

''We drag 'em in, their lawyers pull 'em out. What's to say?'' He stopped talking. In the background a two-finger typist pecked two keys and said, ''Damn!'' Someone had the squad room radio tuned in to a ball at the Hyatt Regency in Dearborn; the reporter was shouting at the top of his lungs to be heard over the music and buzzing crowd noise.

''I'm leaving the department,'' Bloodworth said. ''Today's my last day.''

''Sorry to hear it. God knows Iroquois Heights needs all the good cops it has. Where do you go from here?''

''I haven't thought about it. I don't plan to for a while.

I've got some money saved up. First I'll take a little vacation, but I won't go anywhere. Sleep with my wife. Play with toy planes. Go out and look at a movie. They tell me they talk now. Then maybe I'll sit down and think about what it is I want to do. I sure don't want to be a cop.''

"I know the feeling.'' Once I was virgin. Once I had never killed anyone. Once.

I wished him luck. He thanked me. We didn't have anything to say to each other after that except good-bye, and we made a mess of even that. For a long moment we listened to each other's breathing. Then he broke the connection.

I picked up my drink and went to the window. The first flakes were just starting to come down, spinning out of the black pall above the light, no two alike, spinning down and down toward the smug shiny slickness of the deserted street. Delicate flakes, the first of the first big snow of the long nightmare of winter in Michigan.

"Lose a killer, lose a cop.'' I drank liquor and watched the snow cover the glassy surface stretching on and on into darkness.

About the Author

Loren D. Estleman is a graduate of Eastern Michigan University and a veteran police-court journalist. Since the publication of his first novel in 1976, he has established himself as a leading writer of both mystery and western fiction. His western novels include Golden Spur Award winner ACES AND EIGHTS, MISTER ST. JOHN, and THE STRANGLERS. THE GLASS HIGHWAY is the fourth book in the Amos Walker series, following MOTOR CITY BLUE, ANGEL EYES, and THE MIDNIGHT MAN. SUGARTOWN, the fifth book in the series, was presented the Shamus Award for Best Private Eye Novel of the Year by Private Eye Writers of America. Estleman lives in Whitmore Lake, Michigan.